# A DANGEROUS HEART

Jennifer O'Connor's father died when she was six and her bitter mother always claimed that the Castanien brothers had been responsible. Years later Jennifer, an art teacher, has the opportunity to discover why the brothers behaved so badly towards her father. Max Castanien, now the only surviving brother, requires someone to teach Art classes at his summer house in Umbria. Once there however, living and working near the lovely hilltop town of Montefalco, Jennifer finds herself drawn to Max . . .

LIZ HARRIS

# A DANGEROUS HEART

*Complete and Unabridged*

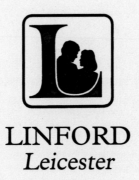

LINFORD
*Leicester*

First published in Great Britain in 2012

First Linford Edition
published 2013

A catalogue record for this book is available
from the British Library.

ISBN 978–1–4448–1539–9

Published by
F. A. Thorpe (Publishing)
Anstey, Leicestershire

Set by Words & Graphics Ltd.
Anstey, Leicestershire
Printed and bound in Great Britain by
T. J. International Ltd., Padstow, Cornwall

This book is printed on acid-free paper

# Memories Are Stirred

The taxi stopped in front of the office block in Holborn. Jennifer paid the cab driver, stepped out on to the pavement and walked slowly towards the building, smoothing down the skirt of her suit as she went.

Her mouth felt dry. She ran her tongue around her lips.

This was the moment for which she'd been longing for the last two weeks; it was also the moment she'd been dreading — she was about to come face to face with the man who'd killed her father.

It was hard to believe that it was just fourteen days since her world had turned upside-down . . .

She'd been leafing through the weekly educational newspaper that she'd borrowed from the staff room. She'd known that she really ought to be marking the final piece of work done by her pupils at her teachers' training placement, but getting a job for September was more urgent.

She went straight to the vacancies for Art teachers, and ran her eyes down the job offers. Her heart sank. Once again the only openings for newly qualified teachers were miles away in the north of England. That was too far from Cornwall. Her mother would be alone if she went and she wanted to be able to come home on a regular basis.

She took a sip of coffee and turned to the last section of the paper where vacancies for private tutors were advertised. A few hours a week as a tutor would be better than nothing until she could get a permanent job.

She skimmed the handful of vacant posts and her eyes stopped. A Max Castanien was advertising for an Art teacher. She sat up sharply, spilling her coffee. This was a name she knew well, a name that she and her mother would never forget.

She spread the paper flat on the desk and stared hard at the name.

Her heart started to race.

She was silly to let herself be so shaken by the sight of a mere name — there was obviously more than one family in the country with that surname, and there was probably more than one Max Castanien. It was highly unlikely that he was one of the Castanien brothers, Max and Peter, whom she and her mother hated so much.

For several moments she sat biting her thumbnail, staring at the advertisement for someone to teach Art classes throughout the summer on a property in Italy. The only other information, apart from the name and brief job description, was a P.O. Box number.

Could this possibly be the same family, she wondered.

She pushed the newspaper aside, pulled her computer towards her and switched it on. She was almost certainly wasting her time, but she couldn't leave it at that — she had to know.

There were bound to be any number of references to the family and their textile business on the internet, and there might just be something there that linked them to Italy. And if the man who was looking to hire an Art teacher turned out to be one of the brothers responsible for her father's death . . .

She could hardly breathe.

If she could just meet him, she might have a chance — a slim chance — of finding out why the brothers had acted as they had done. She'd been too young at the time to remember for herself much about what had happened, but her mother had kept it alive for her throughout the passing years. The Castaniens had brought misery into their lives, and it had stayed there.

But her mother had never really been able to satisfactorily explain the reason behind the men's actions. It wasn't her fault — she probably didn't know everything that there was to know.

However, if she could meet the brothers . . .

Her heart gave a sudden lurch at the thought of learning why the men had let her father down so badly. She felt a momentary shock. She hadn't realised quite how desperately she wanted the answers to her questions.

Several times over the years, she'd thought about writing to them and asking for an explanation, but she'd always instantly dismissed the idea. There'd be no point. They'd have time to compose something which sounded a good answer, but which was unlikely to be the whole truth. But if she could get to know them without them knowing who she was then she might be able to ask them in person.

She mentally shook herself. She was letting herself get carried away. The first step was to find out if this was *the* Max Castanien.

Her heart thudding, she typed his name into the computer. As she'd expected there were several pages of

5

entries. She skimmed down the first page, clicked on a recent interview, and read every word.

When she came to the end of the interview she leaned back against her chair, shaking. When the man had finished answering questions about his role in his local business community, he'd been asked what he did in his free time. He'd told the interviewer that he'd just bought a place in Umbria and was planning to offer Art classes on a second, smaller property on the estate.

It *was* the same man.

For several moments, she stared motionless at the screen.

And what about Peter, she suddenly thought. Peter was the older brother if she remembered rightly, so he was probably the guiltier of the two. Was Peter also involved in the art project? She typed in his name and a list of obituaries hit her in the face.

She drew her breath in sharply — he was dead. He had died after a short illness eleven years ago. She'd been hating him for all those years, and he hadn't even been alive.

Feeling sick to her stomach she clicked on the first of the obituaries and read it. He'd left a wife and a son of eight, Stephen. The obituary had quoted Max's eulogy, word for word. He had spoken movingly about his brother, praising him as an excellent businessman and as a loving brother, husband and father, and he'd ended up by promising that he would always be a strong presence in the life of his nephew, Stephen.

Peter may well have been all those things, she thought in a sudden wave of bitterness, but he certainly wasn't a good friend. And nor was Max.

She glanced at the small photograph of Peter in the corner of the obituary, clicked on it to make it larger, and stared at it long and hard. He'd been nothing out of the ordinary — quite good looking, she thought, but with a weak chin.

She closed the obituary and returned

to the pages about Max. Further down there was an article about the family business, and as she'd suspected there'd be, there was a photograph of him. She enlarged the photo and studied his face. He was definitely better looking than Peter, and he had a stronger chin. In fact, she hated to admit it but he was handsome.

One thing was clear from the photos of the brothers — she'd been wrong in thinking that Peter had been the power behind every action that the brothers took. Despite being several years younger, it would have been Max.

Neither man looked unpleasant, but that just showed how deceptive appearances could be. A person's actions told the truth, and what the Castaniens had done spoke volumes about them.

She sank back in her chair, her eyes still on the screen. It felt very strange, seeing their faces after all this time. She could have looked at their photos at any time over the years, but she'd never wanted to. It had been difficult enough listening to what they had done. Seeing them would have made everything even more horribly real. But now . . . now that there was a chance that she might be able to meet Max in person.

She sat up. There was no time to waste. She must get down to her application letter at once, and it must be good enough to get her an interview. She glanced at the advertisement again, and wondered how best to begin. Having completed the Art teacher training course, she'd had enough teaching experience to know that she was competent to run the classes he wanted to put on, and that must come across in her letter.

And so must her ability to speak Italian. Alongside her main subject, Art, she'd taken Italian as one of her options. The CD of her work, which all the teaching trainees had been advised to send with any job application, would show both her painting ability and her genuine interest in Italy. She'd spent two summers in Florence looking after children, and the paintings she'd managed to do in her free time were among those on her CD.

She bent over the computer. Her fingers hovered above the keyboard, but her mind was blank.

She'd leave the letter until the following day. She'd feel fresher then and less traumatised by what she was planning to do.

She shut down the computer and stood up. As she did so, tears splashed on to the keyboard. She'd put her hand to her face, and realised in surprise that she was crying.

\* \* \*

The Holborn traffic was loud behind her. She glanced up at the tall office block, and her steps faltered. It had all happened so quickly — was she really ready to go through with this?

The day after she'd seen the advertisement, she'd typed up a letter of application, signed it, taken it to the post office and sent it off, confident that he would never recognise her mother's maiden name, which was the surname they'd been using since her father's death.

As she'd walked home, she'd felt a stab of guilt about acting in such an underhand way. But there hadn't been any alternative. And she was doing this for her mother as well as for herself. She wouldn't tell her mother about it, though. There'd be time enough for that if she was successful.

A couple of days after that, her teaching mentor at the school had pulled her aside and told her that her references had been taken up. Her momentary numbness had been followed by a mixture of excitement and fear.

Several days later, Max Castanien's secretary had telephoned to ask if she could come to London for an interview. Apparently, he'd been greatly impressed by the portfolio of work on the disc, the secretary had told her, and by the fact that she spoke Italian.

The gap between the phone call and the interview had passed in a daze.

But she was now in London, about to face him for the first time. She took a step forward, and her heart thumped loudly.

# Meeting The Enemy

Giving her an encouraging smile, the secretary knocked on Max Castanien's door, opened it and stood aside, indicating that Jennifer should go into the office. She took a deep breath, went through the doorway, and hesitated.

'I'm sure you'll be fine,' she heard the secretary say. 'Good luck.' And the door closed behind her.

She took a step forward.

Vaguely, she was aware of a tall, dark-haired man getting up and coming round his desk, his hand held out to her.

'Good morning, Miss O'Connor. It's a pleasure to meet you. I'm most grateful to you for making the effort to come to London.'

Her hand was lost in a strong grip and she found herself staring up into dark brown, fathomless eyes.

'Not at all,' she stammered, her voice seeming to come from somewhere miles away. 'I really want the job, and you obviously wouldn't hire anyone you hadn't met. And you're busier than I am so you couldn't come to me. Not that you'd do so anyway, you're the employer, not me.' She broke off, and went red with embarrassment. 'I'm talking too much, aren't I? It's because I'm nervous.'

He laughed, his eyes crinkling in amusement.

Wow! He's really good-looking, she thought. The photo she'd seen didn't come near to doing justice to him.

'I suggest we sit down,' he said, and he led the way towards a seating area at the side of the room. 'My secretary's going to bring us in some refreshments, and we can talk.'

She went and sat on the dark brown leather sofa. Max Castanien took one of the chairs opposite her on the other side of the glass coffee table. The door opened and his secretary came in,

14

carrying a tray. When she'd finished pouring, she left the milk and sugar, a plate of biscuits and the half-empty cafetière on the table, and went out.

'Help yourself to milk and sugar, if you take it,' Max said, picking up his cup. 'I take mine black. The amount of coffee I drink, it's not particularly good for me, I know, but that's the way I like it.' He settled back in his seat and smiled encouragingly across the table. 'So, Miss O'Connor, I'm curious to know what first got you interested in art.'

She cleared her throat. She was finding it difficult to speak. From the moment that she'd seen his name and confirmed that he was one of the hated family, she'd been hoping for this opportunity.

She cleared her throat again and tried to keep her shaking voice light. 'It's the classic story, I'm afraid. I had a brilliant art teacher in my first year at secondary school and she started me off. I wouldn't have used the word inspiring

15

when I was eleven, but that's exactly what she was. She helped me to discover a talent for painting, and I haven't looked back since then.'

'That's something we have in common, then. We were both lucky with our teachers. As with you, it was a teacher who opened the door to art for me, too. Unfortunately, though, it was for art appreciation only — I was beyond help when it came to the drawing side of things. You should have seen some of my efforts.'

She laughed, her nervousness starting to disappear, and she pulled herself up sharply. Whilst he was coming across as a very pleasant man, from what she'd been told there was another side to him, and she mustn't let herself be blinded by his superficial charm.

He gave her a broad smile and picked up a biscuit.

'I'm curious to know why you chose to learn Italian,' he said, sitting back against his chair. 'You don't look as if there's any Italian in your background

— not with that blonde hair and those blue eyes.'

Jennifer gave an awkward laugh. 'No, there are no Italians that I know of among my ancestors. It was just that we had to pick two options at college. I took the History of Art as one of them, and Italian as the other. I love the work of the Italian Renaissance artists so it seemed a good idea to learn their language, and I'm really glad I did. Thanks to my college I got a summer job just outside Florence. It was brilliant, and the family asked me to go back again the following year, so I really got to practise my Italian. I've made a point of keeping it up since then.'

'Well done, you. You've obviously got real tenacity. I admire that in a person.'

'What about you? Do you speak any Italian? You've obviously got a place there.'

He gave her a rueful smile. 'I've been trying to learn it, but I don't seem to be making much headway. I could blame it on lack of time, but I think it's more about a lack of flair for languages. I'm a businessman, not a linguist and I'm afraid that my attempts to speak Italian are rather on a par with my attempts at painting.'

They both laughed. He leaned forward and topped up their coffees.

She waited with bated breath. If only she'd done enough to get the job. She'd never have another chance like this.

'Look, I don't want to play games, Miss O'Connor,' he said when he'd put the cafetière back on the table. 'You were streaks ahead of the other applicants in the quality of your work, and your references were excellent. What's more, you speak the language.'

Her heart was in her mouth.

'Today was about seeing if we'd get on together. I'll be spending the summer in a house which is only a stone's throw from where the Art classes are going to be held, so I'll regularly be bumping into whoever's taking the class. It's important, there-fore, that we rub along well.'

'Of course,' she said, nodding. She desperately hoped that he couldn't hear the loud thudding of her heart.

'I'm pretty sure we could get on, and the job is yours if you want it,' he said with a smile. A powerful wave of relief surged through her, and she felt weak. 'But don't worry,' he added. 'I'm not expecting an answer this moment. I'm sure you'll want to go away and think about it. Talk it over with your family, perhaps.'

'I don't need to think about it,' Jennifer said quickly. 'From the moment I saw your advertisement, I've not been able to think about anything other than what a marvellous opportunity it would be. Thank you very much, Mr Castanien. You can't imagine how delighted I am to accept your offer.'

His face broke into a broad smile, and he reached across the table, his hand outstretched. All she could see was two broad shoulders in front of her.

He sat back. 'Now that that's agreed,

I can tell you what I've decided. I know I said in the advertisement that the job was to run Art classes throughout the summer, but I've been giving that some thought. My feeling is that it's probably too late now to get a full summer of classes off the ground, especially as I'm short of material that I can use to advertise the courses. I suggest that we treat this as a practice year and run one class only.'

'One class only?' she echoed, her heart sinking.

'Don't look so downcast,' he laughed. 'I still want you there for the whole of the summer. I need you there well ahead of the class so that you can organise everything and order what you need. Then you'll run the course for the week, and when it's over, we'll have a better idea of what to offer in the future, and how to plan it and price it.'

'I suppose that makes sense.'

'I really think it's the best thing to do. I've worked out what to charge for the week this year, but much of it is based on guesswork. When the students have gone home, I'd like you to stay on for the rest of the summer and do some sketches of the house and area that I can use for promotional material. It would be a real waste not to take advantage of having an artist of your calibre there. So, what do you think of the idea?'

'I think it sounds amazing,' Jennifer said, fighting back a rising sense of excitement that she ought not to be feeling. The job was only a means to an end. 'I feel as if I've just been given my dream job. Thank you, Mr Castanien. I only hope that I don't disappoint you.'

He gave her a slow smile. 'I don't think you will, Miss O'Connor. I think I've been very lucky to find you. Now, let's talk about dates.'

* * *

Her senses spinning, Jennifer walked out of the building. On the surface,

Max Castanien was charming, personable and very good looking — in fact, he was the sort of man you could easily fall in love with. But she wasn't going to let herself be taken in by what was on the surface.

She must never for one minute forget that he was one of the two men whose actions led to the death of her father. Every time he turned on the charm, she must consciously remind herself of that.

She raised her arm to hail an approaching taxi. If only he wasn't so handsome, she thought as she stepped into the taxi. It'd be so much easier to think the worst of him.

Her ticket for Italy and the travel details came soon after her interview, along with a note from Max telling her that he and his nephew, Stephen, would be arriving at their house shortly before the week-long course began. He added that Stephen had said that he would like to go to some of the classes, but only if she didn't mind.

Of course she didn't mind. On the

contrary, she was thrilled, as it meant that she was likely to meet her employer more often than she would otherwise have done. The more they met up, the greater the likelihood of a friendship developing between them, and to have such a friendship was her aim. Her best chance of finding out what she needed to know lay in the exchange of casual comments between friends.

She'd promptly written back saying that she'd be delighted if Stephen joined the class. She'd paused a moment, and then added that she was very much looking forward to meeting Max Castanien again.

And, indeed, she was.

# Arriving In Italy

The air was filled with the heady aroma of the lilac-coloured wisteria that grew in profusion around the grey stone walls of the Umbrian house.

Jennifer paused in the middle of arranging several chairs in a semi-circle at the edge of the terrace, and glanced across the garden towards the distant hills. They were shimmering in a haze of blue and purple. On impulse, she left the rest of the chairs where they were and walked along a path flanked by lavender bushes that took her past the pool and out on to an expanse of grass which ended at the top of a steep slope.

She stood and stared at the view in front of her. Neat rows of grey-green olive trees lined the sides of the slope as it fell to the wide plain below. Beyond the trees, a violet haze drifted upwards from the plain, uncovering fields that were painted in shades of green and sunflower yellow. A road, bordered by scattered oak and elm trees, meandered across the plain to distant Bevagna, winding its way past clusters of grey stone houses whose walls and tiled roofs were taking on a golden hue in the rays of the early morning sun. No wonder Max had fallen in love with the area, she thought.

A light breeze swept across the side of the mountain and she felt the coarse grass tickle her bare toes. Looking down at her feet, she saw that her sandals were damp where they'd brushed against the dew-tipped poppies and grape hyacinths that were growing among the grass.

Jennifer glanced up and stared again at the view. A wave of sadness swept through her. She was about to spend two months in a stunning place, and she should be looking forward to relaxing and spending a blissful summer doing something she really loved. Instead, she was a mass of muddled emotions. If only her family and the Castaniens had never met . . .

She mentally shook herself. She mustn't think like that. They *had* met, and she'd come to Umbria for one purpose alone. Fulfilling that purpose had to be her top priority.

No, not her top priority — it had to be her only priority. That was the sole reason she was there. The rugged appeal of her boss, the beauty of the place, the thrill of her first paid teaching job — all paled to insignificance next to the goal that had brought her there.

With a last glance at the panorama in front of her, she turned round and walked quickly back to the house. When she reached the terrace, she shook some loose gravel out of her sandals, picked up the chair nearest to her and added it to the semi-circle.

'Do you want a hand?' a female voice called.

Looking up, she saw a red-haired girl emerging from the patio doors. 'It's

OK, Clare. I'm fine, thanks. But it was nice of you to offer.'

'I don't mind helping, if you want me to.'

'It's very kind of you, but I've done it now. It wasn't exactly demanding — a chair for each of the six of you, one for me, a table, an easel and some equipment.'

'There are only five of us. At least, there were only five of us at dinner last night, not counting you.'

'There's a sixth, but I don't know whether he's joining us this morning or not. He and his uncle arrived from England late last night. They're over in the main house. You can just about see it if you look over there.' She pointed towards the row of tall dark cypress trees which ran parallel to the house, down the side of the garden to the top of the slope. A stone house could be glimpsed in the distance through the trees. 'Both of the houses belong to Mr Castanien. His main home is in England, though.'

'He owns all this? Wow! Is he tall, dark and handsome? Forget that! Is he married or single? And what about the nephew?'

Jennifer pushed a smile to her lips as she arranged the final chair so that it was facing the other six. She looked at the grouping, and moved the chair back a little, increasing the distance between her chair and the others. Straightening up, her eyes strayed towards the row of cypress trees. Max could arrive at any minute.

Jennifer's stomach was in knots. She went over to her easel and began to pull it to the side of her chair so that it faced the semi-circle.

Clare rushed forward to help Jennifer with the easel. 'Oh look, we've got company. It's Paula.'

Jennifer followed Clare's gaze to a woman with long, black hair who was standing under the leafy awning that shaded part of the terrace. The woman looked briefly around her, then started to walk across to them.

'I hope she's not going to go on all the time like she did last night. She could chat for England,' Clare muttered under her breath.

Jennifer gave an involuntary smile of amusement. 'I didn't hear that,' she said, trying to push all thoughts of Max possibly turning up that morning, to the back of her mind. She hooked a large flip-over pad of white paper to the top of the easel and pulled a low table with a large box on it next to the easel. Running a successful class was an integral part of her plan to get closer to Max, and she would have to be alert to the needs and personalities of the group if she was going to achieve her goal.

Paula reached them and gave a tinkling laugh. 'So this is where the girls gather.'

'Not by design,' Jennifer said with a welcoming smile. 'But the ladies do seem to be the early birds among us.' She bent down, opened the large box and took out a selection of brushes and art paper. Then she straightened up.

'Well, I think that's all the setting up done for now. Have the two of you had your breakfast?'

'I have,' Clare said. 'Not that I ever have much of a breakfast. Coffee's all I can stomach at this unearthly hour.'

'I've eaten, but Howie hadn't quite finished so I left him to it. He won't be long, though. We thought we'd have breakfast by ourselves on our private patio each morning, if that's all right. Being newly-weds and all that,' she added with a little girl laugh.

'Of course it's all right,' Jennifer assured her. 'You're all free to do that if you want.'

'Well, I don't,' Clare said. 'I'd rather have company.'

'Just wait till you're married,' Paula said. She pushed her hair behind her ears, closed her eyes and looked up towards the sun. 'It's going to be really hot today.'

'It certainly looks that way. There was a definite heat haze over the valley this morning,' Jennifer said. She glanced towards the patio doors. 'I shouldn't think that Mr. Rayburn and Nicholas will be much longer. If you want, you can sit down and wait for them to arrive, or you can go for a stroll around the garden. The view is extraordinary at any time of day.'

'Good morning, ladies. Or should I say *buon giorno*! We are in Italy, after all.'

Jennifer turned and smiled warmly at the grey-haired man approaching them.

'Good morning, Mr Rayburn. I hope you slept well.'

'Indeed, I did, dear lady. Like the proverbial log.'

'That's good. I was just suggesting to Paula and Clare that they might like to wander around the garden while we're waiting for everyone to get here.'

'No need!' A tall, slim man in his early thirties hurried out on to the terrace. 'You can tick my name off the list, and also Nicholas's. He'll be out in a minute — he's just finishing his coffee.'

'Did you have enough to eat, Howie

darling?' Paula asked, moving to her husband's side. She clutched his arm and gazed adoringly up at him.

He gave a theatrical groan and rubbed his stomach. 'More than enough, sweetheart. I should have stopped long before I did. You're going to be going home with a very fat husband, if I don't watch it.'

'Then it'll be all the more to love,' she murmured. Smiling happily, they leaned towards each other and their lips lightly touched.

Clare glanced at Jennifer and pulled a face.

Running footsteps could be heard from inside the house, and a young man bounded out on to the terrace.

'I hope you haven't all been waiting for me,' he said, panting hard as he reached them.

Jennifer heard Clare give a low whistle behind her. 'He looks even better in the daylight, Jennifer,' she said in a low voice that only Jennifer could have heard.

Jennifer smiled inwardly — she was getting the strong impression that Clare's mind was not going to be solely on the use of watercolour that week.

'Not at all, Nicholas,' she said. 'You've all arrived at pretty much the same time. Did you sleep well?'

'Fine, thanks. I think I must have been more tired than I realised. I fell asleep the moment I hit the pillow. And you can call me Nick, if you want.' His smile was directed at Clare.

'Right, then. Nick, it is.' Jennifer looked hesitantly around the group. 'Well, we're all here now, apart from Mr Castanien's nephew, that is. But I'm not sure if he's going to join us today. I suggest, therefore, that we make a start. If you'd like to take a seat, I'll begin with a general introduction to watercolour.'

'Who's Mr Castanien's nephew when he's at home?' Nick asked, edging round to Clare's side.

'His uncle owns this house. He and his uncle are in the main house.

Stephen's going to come to one or two classes, but it won't affect what we do.'

She sat down facing them.

A wave of panic shot through her, taking her completely by surprise. Having got through two demanding secondary school placements during her teachers' training course, she'd expected to feel confident in front of an adult class and not at all nervous. But amazingly, she suddenly felt terrified.

Glancing around the semi-circle, she saw that Mr Rayburn was the only one who hadn't yet sat down. He was looking anxiously at his chair. She began to stand up. 'Can you manage, Mr Rayburn?'

He waved her back. 'Have no fear, Jennifer. I'm perfectly fine. I'm just getting my bearings.' He sat down cautiously. 'I'll soon be giving you young ones a run for your money, you'll see.' He nodded cheerfully at the rest of the group.

They smiled politely back at him.

As she sank back on to her seat

again, she noticed that Clare and Nick were sitting next to each other. Not surprising — he was a good-looking young man and Clare was a pretty girl with a lively personality.

Paula was on the other side of Nick, but she had eyes only for Howard, who was next to her. Their every action was punctuated with a loving glance. No surprises there, either — they were on their honeymoon, as they had never tired of telling the group at dinner the evening before.

George Rayburn sat on the other side of Howard, at the end of the row. She noticed that he was surreptitiously shifting his position every few minutes, clearly trying to get more comfortable. She wasn't going to do anything that would draw attention to his need for something with greater support, but as soon as they stopped for coffee, she'd see if she could find him a more suitable chair for the week.

Whatever he had said about keeping up with them, it wasn't going to be easy for someone well past retirement age to keep up with people so many years younger. Their stamina and energy levels were very different from his, and she must try to anticipate any difficulties that he might face.

But that was for the future — it was time for her to begin the first class of the week. She was sure that she'd feel less shaky once she'd begun. Luckily, it looked like being just her and the group that day, and that was a huge relief. She'd feel more up to facing her employer when she had at least one session under her belt.

She took a deep breath and smiled round at them all. 'Welcome to a week devoted to painting in watercolour. It's a fascinating medium, and a much more demanding one than most people think. However, even if you're a complete beginner, you've no need to worry. We're all going to go at our own pace.'

'You're right about it being difficult,' Clare cut in. 'I thought it would be dead easy, but it isn't.'

Jennifer threw her a sympathetic look. 'I remember you saying on your application form that you'd been trying to do some watercolours to hang on the walls of your flat, but had found it very difficult. Hopefully, by the end of the week you'll have some paintings to take back with you.'

'You're going to hang your work on your walls, are you? Oh, how sweet,' Nick said with a grin. Clare blushed. 'No, I think that's really cool,' he added quickly. He threw her an apologetic smile, and she blushed more deeply. This time with a tinge of pleasure, Jennifer noted.

'Don't worry, Clare. We'll cover all the points you need to know during the week. Not surprisingly, though, we're going to start with the basic techniques today — the different kinds of paper we can use for watercolour, the brushes, and so on. Then we'll have a short break for coffee, and perhaps you'd like to have a stroll around the garden.

When we regroup, I'll demonstrate how to do a quick watercolour sketch.'

'Will we be doing any painting today?' Paula asked.

'If you want to do something on your own, of course you can. You'll have seen from the programme I gave you last night that this afternoon's free. You can spend it how you want. You may also recall that I suggested you might like to go into Montefalco later on. It's a lovely little hilltop town, about ten minutes' drive from here. There's quite a steep climb through the new town to get to the old part, but we can take the mini bus and park just outside the old town wall. From there, it's just a short walk up to the *piazza*.'

Out of the corner of her eye, she saw the look of relief that crossed George Rayburn's face.

'The *piazza* in the centre of Montefalco is shaped like a star,' she went on, 'which is unusual as *piazzas* go. All of the narrow lanes leading off it have stunning views.'

'Are there any shops there?' Paula asked. 'I want to take something back for Howie's mother.'

'Only a few, I'm afraid, and most close in the afternoon for two or three hours. You'd do better to wait till later in the week, Paula.' She smiled round at them all. 'Of course, if you'd prefer to stay here, that's absolutely fine, too. You did a lot of travelling yesterday and you're probably still quite tired.'

'I notice, Jennifer, that you've omitted to mention the red wine for which Montefalco is so well known,' George Rayburn admonished her, waggling his index finger.

She laughed. 'So I did, Mr Rayburn. And I also forgot to mention the internet café. It's on the left, just before you reach the *piazza*. You'll see some chairs and tables on the terrace in front of it. I think it's open today if you want to e-mail anyone at home. It's cheaper than using your mobile. And there's a car hire place next to the internet café, so if you feel you need to escape before the week is over . . . '

They all laughed.

'Hey, we've got visitors!' Howard exclaimed, sitting up and staring across the terrace to the house. 'They must have used the path that links the gardens — we noticed it yesterday when we had a late-night stroll. I'll bet one of them is destined for the empty chair.'

Jennifer turned to see Max Castanien walking across the grass towards them, a younger man at his side.

Her heart began to thump fast — this was it.

Every single meeting, every single word, was going to count if they were to become friends. And they must. It was the only chance she might ever have of learning the truth about her father's death.

Her heart was pounding as she rose from her seat and went forward to greet the two men.

# Challenging Characters

'As forewarned, Miss O'Connor, this is my nephew, Stephen.' Max Castanien gestured to the young man at his side.

Stephen pushed a lock of light brown hair back from his forehead, beamed at Jennifer and stepped up to her to shake her hand. She shook hands, subconsciously registering that he had a firm grip, just like his uncle, and that while he resembled his father, he had his uncle's chin. Then she turned to the group.

'I'd like to introduce you to Mr Castanien, who's responsible for the fact that we're able to be here in these lovely surroundings, and to his nephew, Stephen,' she said brightly. 'Stephen is going to come to some of the classes. That's right, isn't it, Stephen?' She directed a welcoming smile at him.

'Well, sort of. Actually, originally I

was only going to go to one or two classes, but I've just changed my mind and I'd like to do the whole thing, if that's OK with you. I can't draw for toffee, but I think it could be fun.' His eyes were on Clare as he spoke.

'Join the club,' Howard called. 'Just wait till you see how awful I am! I'll make everyone else look brilliant.'

In the laughter that followed, Jennifer felt herself unwinding. The worst was over now. She'd met her employer for the second time, this time in a less stressful situation, and it hadn't been too bad. In future, she'd be able to relax more easily.

'Why don't you take the empty chair next to Clare, Stephen? I'll let everyone introduce themselves in their own good time.' She turned to Max. 'Would you like to stay for a while, Mr Castanien? It would be easy enough to pull up a chair for you. I was just about to start running through the basic techniques for watercolour.'

'That's very kind of you, Miss

O'Connor. It's an attractive offer, but thank you, no. We didn't get here till late last night and I've got a number of things to do. If you don't mind, though, we'll both come across and join you for dinner this evening.'

'Not at all. It'll be our pleasure.'

He glanced quickly at the group and then back at Jennifer. 'Are you sure?' he asked, lowering his voice. 'You're only just beginning to get to know each other and I wouldn't want to interfere with the group dynamics. Tell me honestly if you'd prefer us not to come. This week, you're in charge of what goes on in this house, not me.'

'Please, do join us for dinner tonight, Mr Castanien. Stephen's now a member of the group anyway, and I'm sure that we'd all like to get to know you better.'

'It's very kind of you to say so, even though it's probably not strictly true,' he added with a wry grin. 'But I've one or two reasons for wanting to join you. The main one, obviously, is to have a pleasant evening in good company, but also I'm curious to know what sort of people come on a course like this. I need to understand the nature of our potential clientele.'

'Naturally. It'll tell you how to focus the marketing next year.'

He nodded, turning to leave. 'We seem to be on the same wavelength, Miss O'Connor. As far as Stephen's concerned, however . . . ' He looked around for Stephen, and his face broke into a broad smile. 'I'm not sure that my nephew's motivation for wanting to eat here this evening is quite the same as mine.'

Jennifer followed the direction of his eyes. Stephen was sitting next to Clare, gazing at her with puppy dog longing.

She burst out laughing. 'Whatever your motivations, I look forward to seeing you both this evening.'

And she did.

Her best hope of getting close to the man was most likely to be in the evening when he was relaxing after a lovely meal accompanied by a good wine and lively conversation. At times like that, tongues were loosened.

With a jerk, she suddenly realised that he was talking to her again.

'So if it doesn't sound too forward, Miss O'Connor, since we're going to be seeing a fair amount of each other this summer, perhaps you'd call me Max. This is not a location in which to be formal.'

Her heart leapt!

'Of course, I will. Please call me Jennifer.'

He smiled into her face, his dark eyes warm. She caught her breath. 'And now I really must get off. Don't forget, if anyone needs anything, tell Maria. It's her job to look after you.'

'I will. Yes, of course.'

'She'll be here daily from before breakfast till after dinner, apart from the afternoons. The others will have to go through you to her as she doesn't speak English, which you'll have obviously found out by now. But she does understand wild gesticulations,' he added with a laugh. 'That's how I communicate with her and with Carlo. Carlo's her husband, by the way. But again, I expect you already know that, and you'll know that he's the one who'll drive the minibus for you.'

'Yes, I do. That'll work out really well. Thank you.'

'I'll leave Stephen with you now. He'll come back over when he's ready. As for tonight, we'll come across at about eight, in time for the pre-dinner drink on the terrace. See you later, then.'

He raised his hand in a slight wave, and went back across the terrace towards the line of cypress trees.

She stared for a moment at the spot where he'd stood. Then, trembling slightly, she turned back to the group. 'Now, where was I?' she said. 'Oh, yes, the basics of watercolour. Yes, that was it.' She leaned forward in her chair and began her lesson.

★  ★  ★

Jennifer sat under a parasol outside the small café at the edge of the *Piazza del Comune*, licking her ice-cream while she waited for the class to finish looking around Montefalco.

She could hear George Rayburn making appreciative noises inside the café as he sampled the variety of red wines that she'd asked for on his behalf.

'It's my intention to take a bottle of the Sagrantino back to England with me, dear lady,' he'd told her as they'd made their way across the *piazza* to the café after saying goodbye to Howard and Paula, who were off to explore. 'But before making any purchase, I need to ascertain that the wine I buy is the best of its kind for the price that I wish to pay.'

'Just remember the flight weight restrictions, Mr Rayburn,' she'd cautioned him. 'And also that you want to enjoy your dinner this evening,' she'd added with a little smile.

'I can assure you, Jennifer, that I know my own capacity and intend to

47

stay well within it. But I thank you for your concern.' He'd given her a little bow and led the way past the signs that advertised wine-tasting and into the dimly lit interior of the café.

When she'd explained George's requirements to the vintner, she'd bought herself a vanilla ice-cream, having firmly declined George's offer to pay for it, and had gone and sat outside.

As she bit into the sugar cone, she wondered what Max was doing that afternoon. He might be working or he might have decided to have a swim. She'd seen a large pool at the side of his house when she'd taken a stroll around the garden one evening not long after she'd arrived, and she could just imagine him streaking through the clear water, the sunlight catching the droplets that fell from his shoulders.

A loud 'Bravo!' from within the café broke into her thoughts, and she snapped out of her reverie. Whether or not Max was enjoying the afternoon was up to him. More importantly, George Rayburn was having a good time.

And Paula and Howard were bound to be enjoying themselves, too — the two of them alone, wandering around a beautiful little town, surrounded by the scent of flowers and the singing of birds. What more could any honeymoon couple ask for?

It was the other three she wasn't too sure about.

The visit to the Church of San Francesco, which was now a museum, could hardly have been described as an out and out success. While Howard, Paula and George had been listening with apparent interest as she'd led them along a sequence of large frescoes, Nick, Clare and Stephen had been escaping through the back door. They'd disappeared long before she was half-way through her talk.

She took another bite of the cone. It was a timely reminder that they weren't students of art history — they were three young people who'd thought it might be fun to have a week in Italy learning how to use watercolours. But that didn't mean that they were automatically going to be interested in mediaeval art, or in any other sort of art for that matter.

And the same could be said of everyone in the group. Although the Andersons and George had seemed to enjoy the frescoes and paintings that afternoon, she mustn't make the assumption that they'd want to go to a gallery or museum in every town they visited.

When she got back to the house, she'd look again at her plans for their visits to Bevagna and Assisi. The balance between activities had to be correct. Perhaps she'd tell everyone in advance what there was to see, and let them decide about what to do when they got there — they could either wander around with her or go off on their own to see what interested them.

That's what the week was about, after

all. As Max said, it was a learning week, and as with anything new, there was bound to be an element of trial and error.

In a way, the present group were guinea pigs — by the time that there was another group, they'd have a better idea of what to do. But that didn't mean that the first group would be short-changed — on the contrary, they'd probably get more than they'd expected, and perhaps more than they'd even wanted. But with the groups next year . . .

She stopped short. There wouldn't be a next year as far as she was concerned. She was there to find out about Max Castanien's role in the death of her father. Once she'd found that out, she'd be off. She and her mother would move on, and the Castanien family would be consigned to the past. In other circumstances, she might have found Max extremely attractive, but in this matter, there weren't any other circum-stances.

She felt overwhelmingly bleak.

The sound of laughter reached her across the *piazza*. Looking up from her ice-cream, she saw Nick and Clare emerging from one of the lanes, laughing together. A moment later, Stephen appeared behind them. Nick and Clare were the only ones who seemed amused, she noticed. Stephen looked distinctly miserable as he trailed after the other two.

A twinge of uneasiness ran through her. She didn't like the look of the situation that she could see developing between the three of them. She must keep an eye on them and stop wasting her time thinking about Max in a way that she shouldn't.

Two men after the same girl was never good news. It was even worse when one of the men was a paying customer, whose enjoyment of the week was a prime consideration, and the other an outsider — but an outsider who just happened to be the owner's nephew.

If Stephen became really unhappy, Max would soon pick it up, and if he became annoyed by the situation, he might hold her responsible. If he did that, it would be harder for her to get as close to him as she needed to be. She had to do something about the situation — and fast. But she couldn't imagine what.

'Are we the first to get back?' Nick asked, throwing himself into the chair opposite Jennifer. Clare sat down between them. A moment later, Stephen reached them and took the last chair.

'Not quite. Mr Rayburn is inside the café, tasting some of the red wines.'

'Did I hear someone take my name in vain?' George said, emerging from the café, his cheeks heightened in colour. He beamed around the table. Stephen got up quickly, pulled a chair from the next table into the space between Nick and Clare and helped George into it then he sat down again. Nick glanced quickly at George and gave Clare a wry smile. She went pink and looked away. Stephen glared at Nick.

'Did you find a wine that you wanted to buy, Mr Rayburn?' Jennifer asked.

'Alas, I fear that the Sagrantino may well prove to be beyond my purse, Jennifer, and I will have to go for a good, but somewhat inferior, wine. However, that charming vintner is going to bring in a bottle of a very special Sagrantino for me to taste. I told him that I'd return on Friday, and he understood my assurance that I'd definitely be back at the end of the week. It's quite amazing how the language of *vino rosso* transcends linguistic differences.'

'I'm sure it is,' Nick murmured.

Clare smothered a laugh.

'Where are the other two — Paula and Howard?' Stephen asked, looking around. 'I haven't seen them since the museum.'

Nick laughed. 'Don't you mean, *Where's Howie darling?* That woman!'

This time, Clare didn't attempt to

hide her amusement. Stephen glanced across at her, then looked down at the ground.

Jennifer felt an increasing irritation with Nick. He was proving to be rather too full of himself, and getting more so with every passing minute. If he continued to poke fun at other members of the group in their absence, she'd just have to tell him that it wasn't appropriate to do so.

She fervently hoped that it didn't come to that. If she was put in the position of having to tell him off, in effect, it would call for a delicate balancing act. She could easily annoy him by ticking him off, they were about the same age, but at the same time, she couldn't allow anyone to be subjected to ridicule, however gentle that ridicule, and however unaware of it that person may be.

As for the Nick and Clare thing, there was really nothing she could do about it at the moment. Much as she'd like to see a smile return to Stephen's face, and was very anxious that Max didn't blame her for Stephen's low state of mind, she couldn't really do more than hope that Clare, who seemed a very nice girl, would begin to get fed up with Nick's behaviour and gradually gravitate towards Stephen.

'I've not seen them for a while, either, Stephen,' Jennifer replied. 'When we came out of the museum they went back down the hill we'd come up when we left the minibus. They said that they were going to walk around the perimeter of the town and stop at the churches of each of the eight saints who were born here.'

'Good grief!' Nick exclaimed, exaggerated horror on his face. 'Sooner them than me. What a way to spend a honeymoon.'

Stephen stared at him in open dislike. 'So looking at what a town has to offer is boring for you, is it? Well, at least that explains why you suggested leaving the museum when you did. You were ready to get off before we'd been there hardly any time at all. Why come out this afternoon if you didn't want to see anything? You might just as well have stayed back at the house and gone swimming or read a book. Assuming you're literate, that is.'

'Ouch!' Nick exclaimed with a wry laugh. 'There's nothing wrong with not wanting to trawl around church after church, is there? In fact, it's perfectly normal. At our age, that is. If that's your thing, Stephen, then you're the oldest twenty-year old I've ever met.' He turned to Clare. 'I bet you're no keener on a load of old churches than I am, are you, Clare?'

'So where did the three of you go after you'd left the museum?' Jennifer cut in quickly.

She glanced at George Rayburn and was relieved to see that his head had fallen forward on his chest and he was fast asleep. It wouldn't have been very pleasant for him to have had to listen to Nick and Stephen having a go at each other at every available opportunity.

'We had a look around the place,' Nick said. 'Then we went to the internet café and e-mailed home. It's just as well that there were instructions in English on the wall. The man in charge of the café didn't know a word of English.'

'I said they could use Uncle Max's internet, but they didn't want to.'

'That was a kind offer, Stephen, but I think they were right to opt for the café. We must try not to disturb your uncle in any way. The art course is totally separate from the main house. Ah, look, Howard and Paula are on the way now!'

They all glanced towards the *piazza* and saw the Andersons hurrying towards them, holding hands.

'I can't wait for the first marital tiff,' Nick muttered under his breath. Clare giggled.

'I do hope we haven't kept you waiting,' Paula simpered with an apologetic smile as they came up to the table. 'Howie and I walked all the way round the outside of the town. It was wonderful, wasn't it, Howie?'

'Yes, it was. But it was hot work and we didn't even stop for an ice-cream,' Howard added, exaggerated woe in his voice. 'Would it be OK if we got one now, or are you all dying to get off?'

'Go right ahead. There's plenty of time,' Jennifer said. 'The ice-cream's simply delicious, I can vouch for it. I had the vanilla.'

'What about you, Clare? Would you like an ice-cream?' Stephen asked, standing up. 'I'm going to get one.' .

'Yes, please. That sounds really nice. Strawberry, if they've got it. If not, I'll have the vanilla, like Jennifer.'

'I think I'll have one, too.' Nick got to his feet.

Paula started to lead the way to the door of the café, then stopped. 'It's suddenly occurred to me. What's the Italian for ice-cream, Jennifer? Howie and I don't know a single word of Italian.'

'I should just stick to *gelato,* which means ice-cream, and *per favore,* which means please. That should do the trick,' she laughed. 'Stephen, you'll need *fragola*, which means strawberry, or you can just point at whatever's pink.'

'OK, then. Off I go. Be prepared for anything, Clare,' Stephen grinned.

Chorusing *gelato* and *per favore*, they went into the shop, leaving George, his eyes still closed, Clare and Jennifer outside.

Clare jumped up. 'You know, I think I'll go after them. This could be quite amusing.' And she followed the others into the café.

George Rayburn stirred, opened his eyes and looked around him.

'They've gone for an ice-cream, Mr Rayburn. Are you tempted to join them? It's a hot afternoon.'

'I am not, dear lady. The pleasure of the wine that I tasted is still with me, and I have no wish to corrupt it.' He paused a moment. 'It's not the easiest of situations, I fear.'

She stared at him in surprise. 'What do you mean?'

'Two men and one young lady. The mathematics don't really add up, do they?'

'I thought you were asleep.'

He lightly tapped the side of his nose and smiled. 'It seemed the easiest thing to do. You didn't want to be worrying about what I might be thinking.'

She coloured slightly. 'That was very considerate of you, Mr Rayburn. Thank you. I'm going to have to stamp on the situation before it goes any further, but it won't be easy. To be honest, I haven't any idea how I'm going to set about it yet.'

'I fear that Nick is a very determined young man, who is not used to listening to the advice of others. But Clare seems a pleasant young lady. It would not surprise me if she didn't soon begin to find our Nick a little too abrasive for her taste. We can but hope so.'

'You're very observant, Mr Rayburn.' She smiled at him. 'In fact, you're quite the dark horse, aren't you?'

'Advanced years do bring with them

some advantages, albeit not that many. You, on the other hand, are very young for such a responsibility. There isn't much that I haven't seen, dear lady, and if I can be of any help at all at any time, you mustn't hesitate to call upon me.'

'Thank you very much, Mr Rayburn. I won't forget your kindness in making that offer, but I hope that I don't have to take advantage of it.'

'As I say, I think that you'll find that Clare solves the problem for you — she seems a sensible young woman to me. But my offer will remain on the table. I believe that that's the phrase.'

There was a noise in the doorway, and Howard and Paula came out with vanilla ice-creams, closely followed by Clare, who held a strawberry cornet. Jennifer saw that Stephen had bought the same flavour for himself.

'I see you remembered *fragola*,' she told him, laughing. 'And not once, but twice.'

He smiled shyly, glancing at Clare out of the corner of his eye.

She beamed back at him, and his smile widened.

Deciding that they would eat their ice-creams while they walked slowly back to the mini bus, they set off across the *piazza* with Jennifer and George leading the way. Howard and Paula brought up the rear.

Halfway down the hill, Clare suddenly realised that the Andersons were no longer behind her, and she stopped walking and looked back.

They were standing outside the car-hire office next to a grey van which was parked up against the wall of the narrow lane. A man in a mechanic's overalls was talking to them. Whatever he was saying, Paula didn't look too happy about it.

Clare saw her glance at Howard, then nod agreement. The man made another comment, pointed to the van, made a gesture that indicated that he was fed up and went back into the office. Clare quickly turned away and ran down the road to catch up with

Nick and Stephen.

'What's the matter, Clare?' Stephen asked, glancing at her. 'You look really worried.'

'It's nothing really. It's just that Paula said she didn't speak Italian, but she must do. One of the men from the car hire's just been talking to her, and she clearly understood what he was saying. They seemed to be talking about that grey van we passed. But how could she, if she doesn't know any Italian, not even how to say ice-cream? Don't you think that's a weird thing to lie about?'

'You must be mistaken,' Nick said. 'No-one would say they couldn't speak Italian if they could. They just wouldn't. There'd be no reason for it. In fact, they're more likely to say that they can speak the lingo when they can't, rather than the other way round.'

'Could you hear what they were saying?' Stephen asked.

'Not really. I was too far away.'

'Well, that's it, then.' Nick smiled in triumph. 'The computer instructions were in English, weren't they? And so were the car-hire details which were also on the wall. We know that the man in the internet café doesn't speak English, so I bet it was the car-hire man who wrote them down. He must speak English.'

Stephen nodded in agreement. 'What Nick says makes sense, Clare.'

Clare's face cleared. 'You're right, it does. No-one would lie about such an unimportant thing.'

A moment later Paula's sandals came clattering behind them on the cobble-stones.

'You're definitely right,' Clare repeated. 'It'd be such a pointless lie.'

# Getting Closer To Max

Jennifer lingered beneath a mulberry tree at the side of the terrace and watched them.

Max was standing at the edge of the terrace looking cool and relaxed in well-cut chinos and a pale grey open-necked shirt. He had a glass in his hand and was staring out at the garden. Stephen hovered restlessly at his side, his back to the view, his eyes riveted to the patio doors. Every so often, Max looked round at Stephen and said something to him. Each time, though, he had to nudge Stephen and repeat what he'd said before Stephen was able to answer him.

It was pretty clear what Stephen was thinking about.

It wasn't so easy, however, to know what went on in his uncle's mind, she thought.

Max came across as being open and uncomplicated, but from what she knew about him, that must all be a veneer. Unfortunately for her, it was a veneer that seemed to be firmly in place. And from the small amount she'd seen of him, she knew that it wasn't going to be an easy thing to discover what lurked beneath the easy charm that lay on the surface.

And she didn't have unlimited time, which made it all the more difficult.

As far as she knew, he was only going to join them in the evenings. It was true that when the end of the week arrived, all the members of the class would go home and she'd be alone for the rest of the summer, sketching the house and the area around the house, but he might decide to leave for England soon after the others. If he did she wouldn't have had sufficient time to find out why he and his brother behaved so cruelly towards her father, which meant that the part that they'd played in his death would always remain a mystery.

If he stayed on in Italy for at least some of the time that she was there on her own, which was the more likely scenario, she would obviously see him on occasions — she'd have to show him the promotional material she was doing, for a start — but they were unlikely to get beyond exchanging platitudes and discussing her drawings unless they had already become good friends. This made it vitally important that she worked on forging such a friendship in the few evenings that they had together that week, and she couldn't afford to waste a single precious minute.

The patio doors suddenly swung open and Clare came through them, wearing a short yellow cotton dress, her hair a mass of lustrous red curls that gleamed in the reflected light. Nick followed closely behind her.

Stephen made a beeline for Clare. 'Can I get you a drink, Clare?' he asked, positioning himself in front of her.

'Oh, yes, please,' Jennifer heard her say.

He went over to the table at the side of the terrace where several bottles of *prosecco* lay on a bed of ice alongside a glass jug of peach purée, picked up one of the bottles and opened it. When he'd finished mixing two *bellinis*, he carried one of the drinks carefully across to Clare.

Jennifer moved swiftly to the table and helped herself to the other drink. Raising her glass to Stephen, she laughingly thanked him as she hurried across the terrace to take the space vacated by Stephen before anyone else had the same idea.

Max glanced down at her, smiled briefly, then looked back at the view. She followed his gaze across the spotlit garden to the feathery tips of the olive trees, their fragile leaves a deepening grey in the fading light of the day.

'This is truly an artist's paradise, Max. The view from up here is inspirational.'

'It is, isn't it? It looks different in every light, but with the sun setting over the plain as it is now, this is a particularly beautiful time of day. It's my favourite time of day, in fact.'

'I think it's mine, too,' she said. 'It's so calm. But a place like this always holds something for an artist, no matter the time of day.'

'I'm sure you're right about that. I don't remember if I told you in London, but I collect paintings in a small way, nothing terribly grand, and whilst I obviously always enjoy looking at my pictures, there is nothing that can surpass the pleasure I get from a view like this. There's always something new to be discovered.'

'I presume that there's a connection between your fondness for your collection of pictures and the fact that you want to set up some art courses here.'

'I'm sure that's true, but it also owes a lot to my total lack of artistic skill. I really admire anyone who aspires to paint and if I can do anything at all to help those interested in drawing to improve, than so be it.'

Jennifer gave him a sly smile. 'And of course, it's nothing to do with the profitable use of pre-existing facilities.'

Max threw back his head and laughed. 'Well, maybe just a little bit. I am a businessman, after all.'

She tore her eyes away from his face, and forced them back to the view ahead of her. 'Well, whatever the reason, it's a wonderful place to have an art course and I'm glad that you decided to go down this path.'

'Me, too. But you wouldn't believe how many people were against it.'

'Against it? Why on earth would they be against it? It's a brilliant idea.'

' 'You should put on cookery courses', I kept on being told, it's the in thing. But imagine being indoors all day, tied to a hot stove, peeling potatoes, chopping vegetables, when there's all this going on in the world outside!' He gestured to the garden. 'Nope, I told them, it's got to be art classes.'

Who was 'them', she wondered and she took a sip of her drink.

He obviously wasn't married — he'd never have come away for so long without bringing his wife if he had one, and nor had there been any mention of a wife in the articles she'd read online — but there could be a girlfriend. And there probably was. The fact that he ran a successful textile company and had property abroad was more than enough to make him highly eligible.

She glanced up at his strong profile and her heart missed a beat.

And also the fact that he was very, very good-looking. Even if he didn't have a single penny to his name, he would still have been in great demand.

But not by her.

Yes, she recognised that he was an attractive man, but she was never going to allow herself to think about him in such a way. She must not be blind to his true character or it might stop her from finding out what she needed to know. It had been a stroke of luck that he needed an art teacher, and she was going to profit from the contact with him it gave her, but definitely not in a romantic way.

A thought suddenly hit her, and she felt a sharp stab of panic. If he did have a girlfriend, and he probably did, she might be planning to join him at some point in the summer. It wasn't something he would have mentioned at the interview in London, his plans for the summer were none of her business, but if his girlfriend was coming out it was all the more imperative that she find a way in which to develop a friendship with him as quickly as possible.

Inspiration struck.

'You're right,' she said with a bright smile. 'Art classes are much more suitable for this location than cookery would have been. But you're wrong about something you said earlier, or rather, you're wrong about something you implied.'

He looked at her in surprise. 'What do you mean?'

'You said that you didn't have any ability for art.'

'Well, I haven't. I'm absolutely hopeless at drawing and painting and that's an understatement.'

'But you could learn to develop such an ability. It's a myth that you've either got talent or you haven't — everyone can be taught how to draw. After that, it's just hard work.'

'Do you really believe that?'

'I know it to be true. I've seen people start an art class without a clue which end of the brush to hold. I've watched them work hard, lesson after lesson, and in the end, they're absolutely amazed at what they've achieved.'

'Thinking of my past efforts, I find that virtually impossible to believe. I'm afraid, I'm still inclined to subscribe to the natural ability theory. I'm the living proof of that.'

'So put it to the test,' she said lightly. 'Come along to some of my classes and see how you get on. Stephen's going to join us, so you could come over with him. There's more than enough equipment for an extra artist.'

She held her breath.

'I may just do that,' he said slowly. 'You've got me thinking now. It could be good fun, and after all, what have I got to lose? You know, you may just have got yourself another pupil.'

She let her breath out slowly. If Max came to the classes, she'd see a lot more of him. That would be a start, but no more than a start. The others would be there, too. What she really needed was quality time alone with him. She would have to come up with a way of getting him by himself.

Her mind went into overdrive. Then inspiration struck again.

She glanced up at him. 'Returning to the fact that you ignored all advice and chose art over cookery,' she said, injecting a bouncing lilt into her voice, 'for purely selfish reasons, I'm very glad that you made the decision you did.'

'For selfish reasons? That's intriguing.' He looked, amused.

'Yes, definitely for selfish reasons. I wouldn't be here if you'd plumped for cookery, would I? I make a mean omelette, but I'd be hard pushed to stretch that skill for a whole week.'

He laughed. 'You've got a point there. Yes, I think I might have expected a little more for my money, both as an employer and as a punter. Now, if you'd been able to make *tagliatelle al tartufo*, in addition to making an omelette, then we could have been in business.'

'That's your favourite dish, is it?'

'Indeed it is.'

She sighed loudly. 'Sadly, I can't claim to be able to make that. Truffles don't abound in Cornwall.' She let a trace of innocent flirtatiousness creep into her voice. 'It would be well nigh impossible to master something I've never tasted. I wouldn't know what I was aiming for.'

He caught his breath in mock horror and raised his hand.

'We must remedy that, and fast, just in case I ever decide to give in and replace art with cookery. We'll look at the activities you've planned for the coming week and pick a day when the class will be so worn out by the evening that they won't notice if you sneak off and play hooky. Then you and I can go to a place in Bevagna that serves the best Umbrian food.'

Her heart gave a triumphant leap.

But she must watch what she said, she thought quickly. Sounding too eager could be counter-productive with a man who was probably bored rigid by women throwing themselves at him.

'That's very kind of you, Max, but you don't have to, you know. I could order it when we go to Assisi. We're there for the whole of Wednesday so we'll be staying for lunch.'

Smiling, she glanced up at him, and caught him staring down at her. Their eyes met.

'No, I prefer my plan,' he said, and he turned back to the garden with a half-smile. '*Tagliatelle al tartufo* is something to be tasted for the first time when you're with a connoisseur. And quite apart from that, I'd quite enjoy having some adult conversation for a change.'

His last words were almost drowned out by the sound of Clare screaming with laughter. They turned to see what was happening.

Stephen had opened a new bottle of *prosecco* and the sparkling wine had gone all over his hands. To Clare's amusement, he was licking the wine off his skin.

'I rest my case,' Max said with a grin.

Laughter lines crinkled the corners of his eyes whenever he smiled, she noticed. And that was often.

She quickly looked away and caught sight of Nick, who was standing just behind Clare. He was watching Stephen with a supercilious air. She felt a momentary chill and her eyes moved back to Stephen. She smiled vaguely in his direction. 'Stephen seems a very nice boy.'

He glanced back at his nephew. 'Yes,

he's a really great kid and I'm very fond of him, but there are limits as to how much one wants to hear about the million and one forms of social networking that he enjoys, or about his taste in music, and I use the term loosely. No, I'm ready for a change of conversation. Having dinner tonight with the group will be a good start, then having dinner with you alone one evening this week will continue the process.'

'I hope you *do* enjoy the evening. They're a mixed bunch, like most such groups. As with every group there'll be some who are more adult than others, whatever their age, and some who'll be more childish. I'm sure there will also be the bores you wouldn't want to sit next to. It's early days for this group and a bit too soon to know which category the individuals fall into, if any. For your sake, I hope their conversation this evening will be on the more adult side, rather than on the less.'

'Adult or not, I'm grateful to you for

letting me barge into what is, after all, your show.'

'I prefer to think of it as *our* show.'

He raised his hands in surrender. 'OK. I'll go along with it being a joint thing. Excuse me, would you? I must speak to Stephen.'

As he went across to Stephen, Paula and Howard came on to the terrace, arm in arm.

'This is going to be the perfect end to what has been a simply perfect day,' Paula trilled to no-one in particular. She adjusted the white flower in her hair, pulled her light flowery shawl around her shoulders and gazed up at the leafy awning above her. 'Oh, look, Howie! Aren't those fairy lights adorable? So atmospheric. This really is the most wonderful honeymoon.'

He slid his arm around her, pulled her to him and kissed her cheek.

'Yuk!' Jennifer heard Nick mutter.

Stephen glanced at Nick and moved from Clare's side to the *prosecco* table. 'We're having *bellinis* this evening,' he called to Howard and Paula. 'Can I make you one? It's the real thing, peach puree and all that.'

'Sounds good to me,' Howard said. 'We'll each have one, thanks. Mr Rayburn's on his way, too. We overtook him while he was looking at one of the paintings. You could pour one for him while you're at it.'

'No sooner said than done.' Stephen arranged three glasses in a row, spooned a little peach purée into each and picked up the bottle of *prosecco*. Just as he was finishing pouring the wine into the glasses, George Rayburn wandered out on to the terrace.

Jennifer immediately went over to him.

'Good evening, Mr Rayburn. I hope you were able to get some rest after the exertions of the day.'

'Indeed I did, dear lady, thank you. I sat in the shade just outside my room, and before I knew it, it was way past the time that I should have been here. I do apologise.'

'Don't think twice about it. This is a holiday as well as a class. Your sleep will have done you the world of good, and you'll enjoy the evening all the more for it. Now, I think Stephen's made you a drink. We're having *bellinis*, but if you'd prefer something else, you only have to say.'

'No, I'm sure that it will be delicious.' He took a glass from Stephen. 'Thank you, dear boy. Don't you worry about me, Jennifer. I shall go and talk to Paula and Howard now. I've just been looking at the painting that I saw them studying earlier today. It really is a most interesting picture and I look forward to hearing what they thought of it.'

Jennifer watched him go across to the Andersons, then she turned and strolled back to Max who had been talking to Clare. As Jennifer approached them, Clare moved away and went and stood next to Stephen. 'Well, that's all of us here now,' she told Max. 'As I said, we're a mixed bunch.'

'Mixed or not, everyone seems to be

very pleased with everything, with maybe one exception.' He indicated Nick. 'But I think that that's more to do with the girl than with anything else. She seems very pleasant, not to mention attractive, and it's hardly surprising that both young men are smitten. No, you've obviously made everyone feel at ease, and very quickly, too. As I believe I have said before, I was lucky to find you.'

'I'd say that I'm the one who's lucky,' she said, smiling up at him. 'I had to find a job for the summer, and this is way beyond my wildest dreams.'

And she was, indeed, the lucky one, she thought inwardly. But for reasons that he'd never dream of.

'I think we'll have to agree that we're both lucky. So, what did you do this morning after I left Stephen with you?'

'I showed them how to do a quick watercolour sketch. I'm keeping all the drawings I do for you to see at the end of the week. Obviously everyone will take the paintings home that they want to keep, but they might leave some of their work behind. Between what's left behind and what I do in the week, there might be something we can use in the advertising.'

'Sounds good. I must say, I'm very keen to see how Stephen gets on. I've seen his efforts over the years and to date they've been far from impressive. You've certainly got your work cut out with him.' He glanced sideways at her. 'And with me, too, if I do decide to come to a few classes. I must confess, I'm quite tempted.'

She opened her mouth to urge him to yield to temptation, but Maria appeared at the patio doors.

'*La cena è pronta,*' she announced.

'Dinner is ready,' Jennifer translated. She smiled round at the group. 'Shall we go and see what's waiting for us?'

# 'She's A Lovely Person'

Jennifer sat back in her chair, cupping her mug of coffee. She glanced round at the empty table and felt very pleased with herself. She was the only person who'd lingered on the terrace after lunch. Everyone else, including Max, had sped off with their easels and art paraphernalia to find the part of the house or garden that they wanted to paint.

She'd set them the task of practising how to mix watercolour with pastel and coloured pencil, something she'd demonstrated that morning. They'd had time to practise for a little while before the end of the morning, and she was thrilled that they were all so keen to get started again.

And she was also very relieved that she'd persuaded Maria to serve a lunch that was more in keeping with the eating habits of the British than the Italians. When Maria had come to her that morning and suggested an Italian-style lunch of *antipasto* followed by two pasta dishes, one after the other, and finishing with tiramisù, she'd had a horrible vision of the whole class taking to their beds for the afternoon!

Using all of her tact, she'd got Maria to scale down the lunch to a comparatively modest *prosciutto* with melon, accompanied by a classic Orvieto white wine, followed by a large yellow peach, some pecarino cheese and coffee. It had proved to be ideal — delicious, but not so heavy that it dulled their enthusiasm for an afternoon activity.

She glanced at her watch. They would have started on their work by now. She'd let them have a little longer and then go and see how they were getting on. She'd leave Paula and Howard's work till last as she'd seen their drawings that morning, and she'd also give George's work a miss for the same reason. If she had time when she'd seen the work of the others, she would look at theirs again.

She'd follow the same format that afternoon as she'd done in the morning — she'd comment positively on their work, give them some pointers, and then leave them alone to carry on. She must remember to keep an eye on her watch, though, as she had to be back at the terrace in time to set up the boards on which she was going to display their work for the critiquing session that evening.

The plan for that evening was to start by having them discuss each other's pictures, after which they'd have an *aperitivo* and then dinner. She rather suspected that Maria was going to go overboard with dinner since she'd had to reign herself in over lunch, so there was no point in thinking of anything for them to do after the meal.

But as far as the afternoon went, she was very much looking forward to seeing how their pictures were coming along, and to finding out what they'd chosen to paint — their choice of location spoke volumes about their character and interests, and to a certain extent about their ability.

She was particularly interested in seeing what Max had chosen to draw.

It was so hard to know what to make of him.

If it hadn't been for what her mother had repeatedly told her about him and Peter, she would have taken him on face value. She'd have thought he was a man without guile, charming, easy-going, ready to be pleased. A man whose business success hadn't gone to his head in any way. A man she could almost have fallen in love with.

But her mother's words were always there, burning away in the back of her mind, stopping her from being taken in by his attractive exterior, forcing her to keep an emotional distance.

And she wasn't the only person who found Max to be excellent company. Several of the group had initially expressed reservations about Max joining them for dinner — Nick for example, and even Clare, although she'd been less vocal. But George had seemed delighted at the prospect of Max's company at dinner, and Howard and Paula even more so. In fact, she'd been amazed at how keen the Andersons had been on Max joining them, given that they always seemed so complete in themselves and had never appeared particularly eager to join the others.

However, any reservations any of them had felt about him joining them, and any fears that conversation might be awkward in the presence of the man who owned the property, had clearly been swept away long before the end of the meal the night before. Max was great company, and even Nick had visibly been won round.

Furthermore, if any doubts had lingered overnight and resurfaced in the morning, they would have been instantly wiped away at the sight of

Max rolling up with Stephen after breakfast, wearing an old T-shirt and jeans, and carrying an easel and watercolours.

'I thought I'd better not miss any more lessons,' he'd told them, and she'd seen from their faces how pleased they'd been that he'd enjoyed their company so much that he'd come back for more.

He'd placed his chair and easel next to Mr Rayburn, sat down and smiled round at them all. As he'd completed his visual tour of the group, she couldn't help noticing that his eyes had lingered on her.

She'd felt hot under his gaze. Her stomach had fluttered, and for a moment or two she'd felt disorientated.

She'd pulled herself together, she had to, and trying to avoid looking at him more than she needed to, she'd begun to demonstrate the art of painting landscapes. Gradually, she'd settled down, and she'd felt quite relaxed by the time it came to showing them the different ways of applying watercolour and how to mix it with other media. After that, they'd spread out in the garden and begun to work on their own sketches. She'd given them time to make a good start on their basic outline, and had then gone from one to the other, looking at each picture and making constructive suggestions.

As soon as she'd reached Paula, she'd stopped and stared at her drawing in amazement.

If she'd had to predict that one of the group would be flowery and superficial, that person would have been Paula. And she would have been completely wrong. Instead of a pretty little confection that bore no relation at all to the object she was painting, Paula's work revealed her to be a true artist.

'If you decided to take art really seriously, Paula,' Jennifer had told her, 'you could be very good. You have real talent.'

Paula had blushed and simpered. 'Oh, no, I couldn't. Could I, Howie?'

She'd felt a sharp irritation with a woman who clearly had ability, but who couldn't decide upon anything without first checking with her husband. Before she said anything rude, she'd swiftly moved on to Howard.

His picture, too, showed above average skill. But whilst it was technically good, it was more pedestrian than Paula's and lacked the indefinable quality that she'd glimpsed in Paula's work.

'Both of you are very good,' she'd told them. 'Is this the first art course that you've been on?'

'We did art at school. We went to the same school — that's where we met,' Howard had said, and he'd turned back to his painting.

'You must have had an excellent teacher,' she remarked, and went across to George.

If Paula and Howard's technical ability was at one end of the spectrum, George's was at the other. Despite clearly making a great effort, he couldn't draw and he didn't have a natural feeling for the medium.

He'd glanced up at her as she'd been studying his work, trying hard to find something to praise that could be used as a foundation upon which he could build.

'Trouble yourself not, Jennifer,' he'd said with a sigh. 'Not even this comfortable chair, which you have been so kind as to find for me, can help. I'm under no illusions about my skill, or rather lack of skill, so you may cease your mental strain and express an honest opinion.'

She'd laughed. 'You're too hard on yourself, Mr Rayburn.'

'And you are too kind, dear lady. Watercolours were my wife's passion. Our home is full of them. Sadly, though, I doubt that I shall be adding to our collection with a work of my own creation. The talent of the many artists who've captured life in watercolour seems to have quite passed me by.'

'Your wife?'

'Agnes. She passed away a few months ago. It had been her dream to come on a course like this. Indeed, we'd found the details of this course before she died and we'd already started to plan our trip. Unfortunately, it was not to be. I decided, however, to do the course for both of us.' He'd stared at his sketch and smiled ruefully. 'But I'm not too sure what she's making of my efforts so far.'

'She'll see them for what they are. An expression of your love,' she'd said gently. 'I'm so glad that you decided to make the trip, George.'

'So am I, Jennifer. I feel that this will bring closure to the sadness of recent months. But not to the happy memories, I shall always have those.'

Closure. George was not the only person on the course who was looking for closure, she thought, moving away. Hopefully, their time in Italy would achieve what both she and George wanted it to achieve — no, what they needed it to achieve.

She'd started to look for Clare, but had suddenly realised that it was time for lunch.

Jennifer finished her coffee and stood up. They had had long enough to settle back into their work after lunch, she decided. She'd start with Clare, which would probably be the quickest way of also finding Stephen and Nick.

Poor Clare. On the one hand it was flattering to have two men interested in her, on the other, it could become quite tiresome, and this was pretty much what Clare had told her when she'd made a remark along those lines that morning. But the more she saw of Clare, the more confident she was that she would sort things out without causing too much pain for anyone.

She started to cross the terrace and make her way to the spot where she thought she'd find Clare. Yes, she'd do the trio next, and she'd save Max until last.

★ ★ ★

'So why did you decide to come on this course, Clare?' Max asked, squinting at his painting.

She giggled. 'Are you asking me that because you can see what I've done and how pathetic it is?'

'Not at all, and I'm sure it isn't.' He got up and went over to her. Standing behind her, he studied her painting. Then he glanced up at the slope that led away from the side of the house, a carpet of pale blue wild flowers beneath a cerulean sky, and looked back again at Clare's picture.

'On the other hand . . . ' They both laughed. 'To be honest, Clare, it's about as good or bad as my own effort,' he said, and he returned to his painting stool. Clare got up and went across to have a look at his picture.

'Mmm. I see what you mean,' she said. Giggling, she went back to her stool and sat down again. She bent her head sideways to study her work from different angles, and sighed loudly. 'It's rubbish. Even I can see that.'

Max smiled across at her. 'Jennifer can say what she likes about everyone being able to learn how to draw, but I've yet to be convinced. And my feeble scratchings this afternoon are doing their best to convince me that if that's the rule, I'm the exception to it. It'll be extremely interesting to see if we make any improvement between now and the end of the week.'

'Are you coming to all of the classes?'

'I doubt if I'll be allowed to. I fully expect to be flunked as soon as Jennifer sees today's offering.'

They both laughed again.

'Jennifer's nice, isn't she?' Clare said.

He smiled at nothing in particular. 'Yes,' he said. 'Yes, she is. Very nice. She knows what she's doing, and she's good with people. She certainly seems to have admirable patience with everyone.'

'I wish I could draw like her. And I wish I looked like her. I've always wanted long blonde hair and blue eyes. Instead, look at what I've got.' She pulled a red curl in front of her eyes, stared at it with annoyance, then pushed it back from her face.

'You've got beautiful hair, Clare. Don't knock it.' He paused a moment. 'I know I should be focusing on what I'm doing and not distracting you while you're in the throes of producing a masterpiece, but I'm really curious as to why you, and all the others, too, have chosen to come on such a course. I'm glad that you have, but why did you?'

'A moment of madness in my case, I guess. I'm training to be a nurse and the government gives us a bursary every year to help with our degree. It's not a lot of money, but it means that I'm not totally penniless. My mates decided to go to Corfu, but can you see me on a beach all day with this hair?' She pointed to her head.

'Not very easily, I must admit.'

'And anyway, a beach holiday like that would be boring, so I decided to do something totally different.'

'And is it fun?'

'Yes, I'm really enjoying it. I genuinely would like to get better at painting, but if I don't, it's not the end of the world. I'll have had a good time, and that's the main thing.'

'I know it's early days, but from what you've seen, if you could change anything about the week, what would you change?'

She paused a moment. 'I'd have only one cool guy on the course, not two.'

He grinned at her. 'I did rather notice that my nephew's smitten, and, so indeed, is Mr Williams. I'm not going to ask which of them you prefer.'

She blushed. 'They both seem very nice in different ways.'

'That's a very good answer to the question I didn't ask.'

They smiled at each other, picked up their paint brushes and started again on their work.

A few minutes later, Max gave an exclamation of annoyance. 'I can't believe I just did that! Have you managed to mix any pastel with watercolour yet, like Jennifer showed us this morning? I've just had a go and ended up with a multi-coloured blob — a blob that's spreading all over my drawing as I speak.' He grabbed a rag and frantically blotted the paper. 'And now I've made it even worse!'

'Oh, there you are, Uncle. How are you getting on?' Stephen came up behind Max, leaned over him and looked at his work. 'Hmm. Give me a minute or a hundred, and I'm sure I'll think of something nice to say.' He glanced up at the wisteria on the corner of the house, and stared again at the picture. 'Missing that first lesson must be to blame.'

Laughing, he went over to Clare.

'That's ever so good, Clare,' he said, staring at her work in open admiration. 'With your work, I don't even have to look at the view to know what you're painting.'

He glanced back at Max and they grinned at each other.

'I can't tell you how much I'm

looking forward to scrutinising your efforts this evening, Stephen,' Max said cheerfully. 'I'm sure I'll have much to learn from them.'

'I don't think I should show you what I've done. The quality of my work might make you give up on the spot.'

'Ah, but you've no choice in the matter. If you look at today's programme, you'll see that our efforts are going to be on display before dinner. What's more, we're going to have more than one occasion on which to gaze in silent awe at what we've all done — we're critiquing each other's work in the evenings.'

Stephen's eyes narrowed as he looked at his uncle. 'I think you should skip that part of the programme, old man. Any sudden strain could damage your health, and I dread to think what might happen if you became apoplectic listening to the honest comments made about your work.'

Amusement flickered across Max's lips. 'Your concern is deeply touching, dear nephew. However, my aged bones and I will risk it. After all, we have a nurse among us.'

'So we do.' Stephen turned and beamed at Clare. 'But if anyone's going to need Clare to resuscitate them this evening, I want that person to be me.'

Clare went red. 'What did you paint this afternoon, Stephen?'

'The wine-terraced slopes leading down to the valley. It's one of the scenes that everyone thinks of as soon as anyone mentions Italy.'

Footsteps sounded on the gravel path, and Nick came into sight. 'So that's where you've all got to! Jennifer's looking at your work as I speak, Stephen. I told her I'd come and find you. She's just done me.'

'Good or bad?' Clare asked.

'She was lost for words, it was so brilliant,' he said with a grin.

'Huh!' Stephen exclaimed.

'Shouldn't you have gone by now?' Nick retorted.

'You're right. I'm off.' With a wave at

Max and Clare, Stephen started to go back to his easel. 'I'll see you later,' he called over his shoulder.

★ ★ ★

'That was a wonderful meal,' Howard said, rubbing his stomach. 'I'm not sure I'll be able to get up from the table.'

Jennifer laughed. 'Maria had something similar in mind for lunch, too. Can you imagine eating two such huge meals in one day? How Italians manage to stay as slim as they do, I don't know. Not all of them, of course, but the majority.'

Clare sighed enviously. 'They must have magic ways of burning off the calories. I just wish they'd share them with the Brits.'

'You're fine as you are, Clare,' Nick said. He put his arm round the back of her chair. She moved slightly forward and he dropped his arm.

Paula turned to Max, who was at the end of the table next to her. 'Howie and

103

I were saying earlier how flattered we were at you choosing to spend so much of your precious time with little old us.' She tinkled a silvery laugh, took an *amaretto* from the bowl in the centre of the table and popped it into her mouth.

Max glanced towards the other end of the table to where Jennifer was sitting. Their eyes met. They smiled at each other, then Jennifer looked away and said something to George, who was sitting next to her.

Max turned back to Paula. 'All I can say is, I'm enjoying myself enormously. I'm very grateful to all of you for letting me join in. Originally, I'd intended to come over in the evenings only, but I seem to have become a fixture in the day, too. It's certainly a very different week from the one I would have had if you hadn't been here, but it's turning into a most interesting one.'

'What would you have been doing if we hadn't been here? You don't seem to be the sort of person who'd lie by a pool all day long and do nothing,'

Howard said, sliding his arm around the back of Paula's chair and leaning a little closer to Max.

'I'd have a swim before breakfast, and again in the afternoon, but you're right, lying around in the sun is not for me. If you weren't here I'd probably spend more time relaxing on the *loggia* — that's the veranda which runs around part of the house, and it's where I usually eat.'

'It sounds heavenly.' Paula sighed.

'It is. I expect that I'd sit there for longer than I do after each meal, reading or looking at the view. Being on a slope means that there's usually a gentle breeze, so it's all very pleasant. But having said that, knowing me, the truth is I'd probably find it impossible to switch off the work mode and I'd go back to my computer out of sheer habit. I suspect that I'm going to have more of a rest by joining the class than I would have done had I stayed on my own.'

'Your life here sounds idyllic.' Paula sighed. 'Even if you do go on the computer more often than you should when you're on holiday. Don't you think so, Howie?'

Howard nodded. 'Absolutely. Although, if I'm truly honest, I think I'd need a hobby to fill my time. Books are absorbing for only so long. As for working when I'm away, forget it.' He slipped his arm from the back of Paula's chair to her shoulder.

'I couldn't sit and read all day, either. It would become boring very quickly. But I'm extremely lucky. I've got an interest that I can pursue in both England and Umbria. I've been collecting pictures in a small way over the years. It's just a hobby, but one I love, and I've every intention of spending a large part of my time in Italy visiting galleries and exploring little shops in out of the way places. Who knows, I might find a hitherto undiscovered masterpiece,' he added with a laugh.

'Oh, what fun!' Paula exclaimed. 'Isn't it, Howie?'

'It certainly is. I envy you, Max.'

'And galleries and museums aren't the only places one can visit — nearly every church, no matter how small the town, has at least one painting worth seeing. In fact, I'd originally intended to take Stephen around some of the nearby churches this week. Funnily enough, though, just after I told him of my plan, he confessed to a burning desire to join the art class.'

He glanced affectionately at Stephen, who was deep in a conversation with Nick and Clare. His gaze slid to Jennifer. She was listening intently to George, her blonde plait lying across her shoulder.

'Jennifer seems very pleasant, and a good teacher, too,' he said, thinking aloud as he stared at her.

'Oh, she is. She's a lovely person. Howie and I feel that we've already learnt so much from her. I've no idea what your art collection is like, Max, but I think that we're going to have a fine collection to take home with us, too.'

'Are your paintings here or in England?' Howard asked.

Max pulled his gaze away from Jennifer. 'Mostly in England. I've got a few pictures here as well, but my main collection is at home. But don't get carried away and imagine rooms of Leonardos. If only! No, it's only a very modest collection, something I do for fun.'

Howard picked up the bottle of dessert wine, leaned in front of Paula and divided the last of the wine between his glass and Max's. 'What style of art do you go for, Max?'

'I'd say I was quite eclectic, but modern art probably predominates. Certainly the pictures I've got on the walls here are modern. I brought them over from England. For all that these are fourteenth century houses, I felt that modern art would be more in keeping with the style of furniture I've chosen. Classical wouldn't work as well.'

'How I love looking at paintings.'

Paula's voice was tinged with wistfulness.

'From what I saw earlier, you're a pretty good artist yourself, Paula. Your work today was really impressive. Out of all of us, you and Howard are the only ones who seem to have a natural flair. I'm sure you'd be able to sell your work.'

'It's sweet of you to say that, Max, but I'm sure I wouldn't. Who'd want to buy anything painted by little me?' She giggled.

'Paula was told the same thing at school, but it's a difficult business to succeed in and she's never attempted to make it her career. It's always been a bit of a regret,' Howard said, glancing lovingly at his wife. 'Which is one of the reasons we chose this sort of week for our honeymoon. It's a moment of luxury amid the humdrum of everyday life. We'd be bored stiff doing nothing but sitting in the sun by a hotel pool. We've got the sun here, and a pool, but we've something more, too. No, this is ideal for us.'

Max smiled broadly at them. 'I'm glad that it's living up to expectations.'

'Oh, it is,' Paula said tremulously. She paused a moment. 'Can I be very naughty?' she asked in a little girl voice. Pouting, she glanced at Howard, and then back at Max. 'Howie's going to be very angry with me — he said I mustn't ask you.' She stopped and bit her lip.

'Ask me what?' Max prompted.

'If we could take a little peek at your paintings.' Her words came out in a rush.

Howard took his arm from her shoulder, looked reprovingly at her, and then glanced apologetically at Max. 'I'm really sorry, Max. Paula shouldn't have asked you that. Your house is private.' He turned back to Paula. 'You know what Jennifer said when Stephen offered Nick the use of Max's internet — she made it clear that Max's house was off limits. Nick told you she said that.'

'It never occurred to me that you

might need to use the internet. Of course, you can use it if you want to. I hadn't thought about that side of things. In the meantime, though, just ask me whenever you want to come across. And by all means have a look at my pictures at the same time. It's the least I can do. I'm invading your space every night after all.' He smiled at them both.

Howard and Paula glanced at each other. 'That's very sporting of you, Max. Thank you,' Howard said.

Paula was wreathed in smiles. 'Yes, thank you so much, Max.' She turned to Howard. 'Oh, Howie darling! I'm the happiest bride alive.'

At the sound of Paula's loud exclamations of joy, Jennifer turned and glanced at her, and then at Max's face. His expression was inscrutable. She looked down at her plate, and bit her lip in sudden anxiety.

# Alone At Last

Jennifer turned round at the sound of footsteps approaching the table.

'Max!' she exclaimed in pleased surprise. 'I didn't expect to see you again today until dinner. I thought you were going to have a break from us this afternoon.'

'I thought so, too,' he said, sitting down opposite her, 'which is why I disappeared at the end of the class this morning. But you get used to having company and it suddenly felt quite lonely, sitting on my own with my coffee, knowing that you were close by. So I decided on the spur of the moment to hitch a lift with you into Bevagna, after all.' He paused.

'I hope you don't mind,' he added, a trace of awkwardness in his voice.

A wave of pleasure surged through her. They were going to be spending the whole afternoon together. The degree of pleasure she felt took her quite by surprise, but it was obviously just the thought of having some unexpected time in which to get closer to him. It would bring her goal that much nearer to being achievable.

'Not at all,' she said, smiling. 'And I know the others won't mind, either. They were saying at lunch how much they were looking forward to seeing you at dinner this evening.'

'Which reminds me, I didn't get a chance to ask you this morning, but you looked a bit worried at the end of the meal last night. Is everything all right?'

'Everything's perfect,' she said quickly. 'It's just that Paula seemed to be going a bit over the top from where I was sitting, and I was worried that you might be bored. I wouldn't want you to stop coming across to us. That's to say, none of us would. That's all . . . ' Her voice trailed off.

'You needn't worry on that score. It

would take a lot more than Paula to put me off joining you in the day or for dinner. I'm enjoying myself far too much.'

Relief swept through her, and she felt herself relax. Until that moment, she hadn't realised how inwardly tense she'd been since the evening before. 'I'm so glad to hear that. You coming to Bevagna is a bonus for us. You'll be able to add to what I've already told the group — you must know Bevagna much better than I do. I read up about it before I came, but I've only been there a couple of times, and that was mainly to work out how to organise today's visit.'

'You won't need any help from me, I'm sure. Your handouts this morning covered everything imaginable. In fact, I was quite impressed.'

She laughed. 'I shall take that as a compliment. From the short amount of time I've spent with you, I'd say that you're not easily impressed.'

'You make me sound quite formidable,' he remarked with a grin. 'Like a bad guy from a Dickensian novel, or a domineering sort of father who demands impossibly high standards from his children.'

'Dickensian?' She slowly ran her eyes down his face, lingering a moment on his lips. 'I don't think so,' she said lightly. Her look returned to the dark eyes that were gazing at her with open warmth. 'And certainly not like a domineering father.'

'Phew! That's a relief.' There was an imperceptible pause. 'I wouldn't want to be as unreachable as that would make me seem. I wouldn't like that at all, Jennifer,' he added quietly.

Their eyes met across the table, and neither moved for a long moment.

'It's time I got my things ready for this afternoon,' she said and stood up.

\* \* \*

They stepped off the minibus, crossed a small patch of grass and stared ahead of them at the ancient pink and grey stone bridge which spanned the river that flowed around the walled town of Bevagna. Visible beneath the arch, they could see reflected in the clear green water the pillared colonnade of a house on the other side of the bridge.

'Wow!' Stephen exclaimed. 'That's some view.'

'The house that's reflected in the water is the old wash house,' Jennifer told them. 'When we cross the bridge, you'll be able to see where the women used to scrub their clothes. There's a weir there, too. The view from this spot is one of my favourite views of the town. I think it's beautiful.'

'And what a lovely drive that was, Jennifer,' George said, shaking the stiffness out of his knee. 'I'm quite astounded by the number of wineries in the short distance we've travelled.'

'I know; it's amazing, isn't it?' She looked around at the group. 'Well, welcome to Bevagna. Like most Umbrian towns, Bevagna's a small Roman town, which has also got some mediaeval remains.

Unlike most of the other towns, though, it's not a hilltop town. Apart from one or two slight dips, the whole town is on one level.'

'Thank you, dear lady,' George murmured.

They all laughed.

'We're going to cross over the bridge now and go through the gate, which is just one of several gateways into the town. Then we'll walk to the main square, which is called *Piazza Silvestri*. It won't take us long as it really is a very small, town. The whole town can't be more than two hundred meters in diameter.'

'That is small!' Howard exclaimed.

'But there are still lots of things to see, as you know. We talked about what there was this morning. Several of the most interesting places are in the *Piazza Silvestri* itself, so you won't have to go far. Now, you've each got the town plan I gave you . . . '

'Oh, dear! I forgot mine,' Nick cut in. 'I'll have to share yours, Clare.'

Jennifer noticed Stephen turn sharply and glare at Nick. Disappointment clouded Clare's face and she glanced surreptitiously at Stephen. So that's the way the land lies, is it, Jennifer thought. Good.

'I'll point out one or two places on the way,' she continued, 'but for most of the afternoon, it'll be up to you what you see or don't see, and what you draw. Don't forget to allow plenty of time for your picture. As soon as we reach the *piazza,* we'll get our bearings, fix a time to regroup, then split up. I'll give you time to look around, decide what to draw and make a start on it. And after a certain amount of time, I'll wander around and see how you're getting on.'

'Why don't you give yourself a break and leave that agony until this evening?' Nick suggested with a grin. 'Why ruin your afternoon?'

She smiled. 'I'll risk it, Nick, but thank you for your consideration. If you don't forget what we said about composition and colour this morning, I think you'll all be pleasantly surprised by what you achieve, and I shall be in for a treat this evening. We all will.'

'We'll do our best, won't we, Howie?' Paula gave a little laugh and looked around at the others.

'Right, if you're ready,' Jennifer said, 'we can set off.'

'What about our easels and things?' Clare asked as they started to move.

'Carlo's bringing them to the *piazza* for us.' They turned in unison and looked at Carlo, who was busy taking a small pull-cart from the back of the minibus. 'Off we go, then.'

As she turned to lead the way, she caught sight of Paula grabbing Howard's hand and starting to pull him towards Max.

But Max moved more quickly than Paula and a moment later he was walking at Jennifer's side.

'That was a close thing,' he muttered, wiping his forehead in mock relief.

She laughed. 'So you saw what Paula

was up to, did you? So did I. I'm beginning to think that the Andersons are the sort of people who like to be friends with the boss, so to speak. They're certainly all over you like a rash,' she added as they started to cross the bridge.

'I think you're right. Every time I turn round, I'm in danger of tripping over one of them or both.'

'And that didn't put you off coming this afternoon?'

'Not at all. I felt like having some company and I love the town. Compact though it is, you come across something new on every visit. But I must confess, I do have an ulterior motive, one that I didn't tell you about earlier on.'

'You do?'

'Yes. I've ordered a fruit bowl from a man who has a shop here. He sculptures glass and his work is outstanding. I wanted a particular shade of sea-green, and I knew the exact shape it should be. A while ago I told him what I wanted, or, more accurately, I drew a picture of what I wanted — he doesn't speak English. He said he'd make it for me, and apparently it's ready now. I thought I could collect it today and have a look round his showroom at the same time. It's only small.'

'That's a lot of thought to put into a fruit bowl. I hope that the finished product lives up to your expectations.'

'Why don't you come with me and see if it does?'

She opened her mouth to say that she couldn't.

'And don't say that you've got to stay near the others,' he cut in quickly. 'As you said, it's a tiny town, you couldn't be far from them at any time, and they won't be doing any painting for quite a while. We could go to the glass shop and then have a drink in one of the *piazzas*. I often go to a place in *Piazza Garibaldi* and sit on the terrace there. I'd enjoy talking to you about some of the things you've seen in the short time you've been here. I seldom get the chance to discuss anything artistic with someone who knows what they're talking about. After our drink, you can go off and survey everyone's endeavours whilst I have a crack at doing a picture myself. I'm going to draw one of the gargoyles over the main doorway of the Church of San Michele Arcangelo. They're quite striking. So, how about the fruit bowl followed by a drink?'

'It sounds fun. Thank you.'

'That's great.' She heard genuine pleasure in his voice, and she turned towards him. At the same moment he glanced at her. Their eyes met, and their steps slowed.

His skin gleamed gold in the afternoon sun, and she felt a sudden overwhelming desire to touch his face, to run her hand lightly down his cheek, to feel his skin beneath her fingertips. She wanted to look away but was powerless to do so. Slowly her eyes traced his laughter lines, his nose, the slight cleft in his chin. A lock of hair fell over his forehead, and he raised his hand to push it back.

'Jennifer,' he said softly.

She forced herself to look back at the path ahead, and started to walk quickly, her heart pounding. She must stop herself from thinking about him in that way, and she must make absolutely certain that she didn't send out the wrong signals.

'We're almost at the *piazza* now,' she said a few moments later, her voice strange to her ears.

'I've a pretty good idea what George will choose to draw,' Max said, coming up alongside her. 'In fact, I'd put money on it.' His voice was full of amusement.

She smiled at him, hugely relieved that they'd returned to their normal banter. 'What do you think he'll do, then?'

'The frieze above the door of the Church of San Silvestro. There's a small mountain which has got four streams on it and a growing vine. I bet he focuses on the vine. It's meant to represent the Church or God, but I doubt that our George will be thinking about its symbolic interpretation.'

Laughing, she glanced back. Seeing that the others had lingered on the bridge and were still some way behind them, she stopped walking. 'We'd better wait a moment. We're almost there and I haven't pointed out a single thing so far.'

'Come on, they'll be fine. After all, they've got a map. We'll wait for them when we get to the square. To be honest, I'm enjoying being able to talk to you without someone else taking part in the conversation.'

It was a sentiment shared by them both, she thought. But unfortunately, it had to be for different reasons. She felt a wave of regret run through her. But she mustn't let herself forget why she'd come to Italy, not for one minute.

Originally, she'd thought that his coming across in the evenings would give her sufficient time to get to know him. But it hadn't worked out like that — the others all wanted to speak to him, too, and as he was clearly a polite, socially minded man, he obliged them all. In fact, she spoke to him less than anyone else at dinner as she was at one end of the table, and he at the other. Not that it mattered. They weren't alone so they couldn't have had more than a superficial conversation, anyway, wherever they'd sat.

But the week was flying by at a frightening speed, and this was the best quality time she'd had with him so far in which to develop a friendship based on their mutual interest in art. She couldn't afford to waste a precious second. Nothing else came near to being as important as finding out about her father's death.

'Perhaps I shouldn't have told you that I was enjoying talking to you,' Max remarked with a wry smile as they reached the *Piazza Silvestri* and stood at the side of the fountain, waiting for the others to arrive. 'It seems to have been a real conversation killer.'

She gave an awkward laugh. 'Gosh, I'm sorry! I've been thinking what to say to the class before I send them off to have a look around.'

'As I said before, they've got a map. Ah, here they are. And no surprises who's first.'

'What a pretty little town this is,' Paula enthused as she and Howard came beaming up to them. 'It's so sweet.'

Clare, Stephen and Nick followed close behind them, with George only a short distance away.

When he reached them, they gathered around Jennifer.

'Before we go our separate ways,' she said, 'there are just a couple of things to tell you. Carlo will be staying in front of the bar over there. He'll have your painting equipment with him. When you've seen all you want to see and are ready to start drawing, come and collect your things from him.'

They nodded.

Jennifer smiled around at the group. 'Is there anything anyone wants to ask me?'

They shook their heads.

'It's three o'clock now. Why don't we meet here again at six-thirty? That will give you plenty of time to see all you want, and the shops will have been open for a little while in case you want to have a quick browse before we leave. Hopefully, you'll have managed to fit a drawing in, too. I'll try to get round to all of you at some point during the afternoon. Well, Carlo's in position now, so off you go.'

She turned to Max. The others had gone, and they were completely alone for the first time. Despite everything, she felt a frisson of excitement.

# Falling Under His Spell

Jennifer leaned forward and helped herself to a small tomato bruschetta.

'I really shouldn't be eating this,' she said, popping it into her mouth. 'I had a very good lunch, and I know what Maria's got planned for this evening. I shall be enormous by the time that I return to England.'

'I don't think you've anything to worry about,' Max said warmly. Their eyes met across the table. Both immediately looked away.

He leaned forward to take a truffle-topped *bruschetta*.

At the same moment, Jennifer reached for another tomato one. Their hands touched. Sparks of electricity winged up her bare arm, and she pulled her hand quickly back.

'Go on,' he said. 'Have another one. If you don't, I'll feel guilty about eating so many.'

'Oh, all right, then.' Her skin still tingling, she reached for the *bruschetta*. She must pull herself together, and fast.

'Are your parents as interested in art as you are, Max?' she asked, keeping her voice casual.

'I've never really thought about it. They certainly took great care over the pictures they hung on the walls. They didn't have a collection as such, though. And not one of us — not me, not my parents, not my brother — was any good at actual drawing. We're not creative in that way, just appreciative.'

He'd mentioned Peter! This was her moment and she had to take it.

She felt cold all over. How she hated the idea of reminding him that he'd lost his brother, it was a horrible thing to do. But it might be the only chance that she'd have to get him to talk about his family. It was a subject he had to bring up himself and she had to make the most of it.

She made a conscious effort to

conjure up her father's face, haggard and drawn with the stress he'd been under during the last few weeks of his life, and her mother's features, etched with a grief that had lasted so many years, and took a deep breath.

'When I first saw your advertisement, I looked up your company oh the computer. I couldn't help seeing the obituaries about your brother. I'm so sorry, Max. He was very young to die, and Stephen was very young to lose his father.'

'Yes, that was terrible,' he said. 'Really terrible. Peter was eleven years older than me, but despite our age difference, he was my best friend. I joined the family business straight from school, and Peter was there for me every step of the way. That probably made us even closer. Stephen was eight when he died. I've tried to be a stand-in father to Stephen, but I know he still misses his dad. And so do I.'

'I'm so sorry. I shouldn't have mentioned your brother.'

'Yes, you should. He'll always be a very important part of my life, and I wouldn't want him to be forgotten, or to be someone who could only be mentioned in hushed tones. He was a terrific person. But anyway, that's enough about me for the moment. What about you? Are your parents artists?'

'I don't know about my dad, but my mother could have been good. Unfortunately she only painted as a hobby. She was very young when she had me, and she and my father had a lot of financial worries, so there wasn't enough time and money for her to take it seriously.'

'What does your father do?'

For a moment she wondered whether she should end the deception that was beginning to tear her apart, and tell him the truth, but the moment passed. It was just too soon. 'He had his own business. Stephen and I have something in common — my father also died when I was very young. After he died my mother lost any desire to paint.'

'Now it's my turn to say that I'm sorry for asking you something that led to a sad memory.' He paused for a moment. 'But they would have come up at some point — about your father and Peter, I mean.'

She felt suddenly cold.

'Why do you say that?'

He stared into her face. 'Because I want to get to know you better,' he said quietly. 'Until today I've only been scratching the surface. But I want to know more about what's under that surface.'

She relaxed again. 'How funny,' she said, her voice shaking a little. 'I feel exactly the same way about you.' She felt herself start to blush.

'Well, if we're going to scratch some surfaces, how about another white wine? We've got the time.'

'I'll have an apérol soda this time, please. I've still got to have a look at everyone's work, and I don't want to be seeing double when I do my rounds.'

He laughed, and stood up. 'I'll be back in a minute.' He disappeared into the dark interior of the small restaurant.

Jennifer stared around the *piazza*, biting her lip. They'd finally got on to the subject of their families, which was a huge leap forward, and he'd shown a real interest in her as a person. She couldn't have asked for the afternoon to have gone better. So why did she feel so flat, she wondered.

Max returned to the table, closely followed by a waiter who was carrying a tray of drinks.

He sat down. 'I've asked for some more of the *crostini* with wild boar *paté,*' he said as the waiter put their drinks in front of them. 'I'm having the same as you ordered, it looks a refreshing drink.'

'Did you make yourself understood in there?' she asked, smiling brightly.

He laughed. 'That's something we'll soon find out. I certainly hope so. I know that *cinghiale* is wild boar, but if they didn't understand *paté,* we could have a problem of enormous dimensions on a tiny bit of toasted bread. Cheers.' He raised his glass to her.

'*Salute*,' she reciprocated, and took a sip of her drink. 'Are you planning on spending a lot of time in Italy? After all, you seem to be treating your house as more than just a holiday home, putting good paintings on the walls and making sure that everything is just so.'

'I hope to come over several times a year, even if I can only stay for a few days at a time on some of the visits. I intend to stay for the whole of every August, though, and I see the art courses as being one of the highlights of the summer.'

'Even with people like Paula in them? What were you talking to her about last night? If it was something personal, tell me to mind my own business.'

'It wasn't personal at all. She wants to look at my paintings. She knows that the main collection is in England, but she's still undaunted. I think she also wants to use the internet — either she or Howard brought the subject up.'

'That's so naughty of her. She knows that your house is off-limits. I told them so at the start of the week. What did you tell her?'

'To let me know when she needs to check her e-mails, and she can see my pictures at the same time.'

'That's very kind of you, Max, but you don't have to allow it. I can talk to them.'

'It's nothing. I really don't mind.' He leaned closer to her. 'But what's far from nothing is the fact that I promised to take you to a local restaurant to sample their *tagliatelle al tartufo*. I haven't forgotten.'

She laughed. 'Don't worry, I won't hold you to your promise. We were just joking around.'

'Isn't there a saying, Many a true promise is spoken in jest?'

She laughed again. 'If you say so.'

'I do. A promise is a promise and we shall go.' She opened her mouth to speak, but he held his hand up. 'Stop! I can anticipate you. Go, we will, but not while the class is here. It's pretty obvious that you can't leave them for the whole evening. You're the one who's holding the different elements together, and you need to be there. I shall just have to be patient.'

'So when do you suggest that we go, then?'

'On Saturday evening. The group will be leaving at different times throughout the day, depending on the time of their flights and where they're going, but they'll all be gone by the late afternoon. You're bound to be feeling a bit lonely when they've gone, and so will I, actually. Going out to dinner together will be the perfect way to end the week.'

'What about Stephen?'

'There's enough to keep him amused at the house. If he's truly desperate, he could resort to making a start on his exam revision. So, is that agreed?'

She looked up from her drink and stared at him. In the depths of his eyes, there was unmistakable admiration. But there was also something else. Her heart turned over.

'Yes, it is. Thank you. I'm already looking forward to it.'

And she realised that she was.

# In Too Deep

Jennifer stared in satisfaction at the collection of watercolours arranged around the perimeters of the terrace. She felt shattered, and very relieved that she'd decided against displaying the work they'd done in Assisi that day.

Showing them some well-known traditional and contemporary watercolours was going to be much easier all round. Critiquing each other's work was anything but relaxing for the group, and it was downright exhausting for her. The only person who probably wouldn't be worn out that evening was Max, who'd stayed at home. The rest of them had spent most of the day walking around Assisi, and what they needed was a peaceful few hours in which to recharge their batteries.

'Aha, here you are!' Nick said cheerfully, coming out on to the terrace. He stopped and looked around him. 'So this is the exhibition for Wednesday, is it? I note that it's of a slightly higher standard than on previous days. Delete that. After further inspection, it's of a much higher standard than on the last few evenings.'

She took a deep breath and summoned up every ounce of energy that she could. 'Hello, Nick. It's unlike you to be the first here.'

He grinned at her. 'I like to be unpredictable.'

She laughed. 'I see. It's all part of your allure, is it?'

He gave her a rueful grin. 'I used to think so. Now I rather fear that allure has faded a bit.'

'I won't pretend that I don't know what you're talking about. Cue for a drink, I'm inclined to think. Why don't I pour us a drink and you can tell me about it? If you want to, that is.'

'You sit down, I'll do the pouring.' He filled two glasses, handed one to her, and they sat down at the end of the

139

dinner table, which had been set up outside under the awning. 'I guess it's pretty obvious that he's won Clare's affections.'

'I did notice that he and Clare disappeared as soon as we got to Assisi. It's a shame for you, Nick, but I'm afraid that one of you had to lose out, if not both of you. After all, there was no guarantee that Clare would feel anything for either of you.'

'I know that. But to concede defeat to someone younger than I am, who's still at university — it's pathetic. Mind you, he's got a load of dosh behind him — he's not exactly a student struggling on a pittance.'

'You don't think that Clare . . . '

'No, I don't. Not at all. It sounded as if I do, but I don't. Clare's not like that. I'm just enjoying piling on the agony. Call me a masochist, if you want.'

'It's a pity that there isn't a second unattached female on the course,' she said sympathetically.

'You can say that again. Although, come to think of it, there is.' He grinned at her. 'There's you, Jennifer.' She started in surprise. 'You must be about a couple of years younger than I am, and that's the perfect age difference. And you're very pretty. Yes, the more I think about it, the more I think you'd be ideal for me.'

She laughed awkwardly. 'Slow down, Nick. I'm here to teach, and that's all. I've no hidden agenda.'

But she did have a hidden agenda. Her guilt at having to lie to Nick prickled, and she took a hasty sip of her drink.

'But I'd fail there, too, wouldn't I?' he said, carrying on as if she hadn't spoken.

She looked up, startled. 'What do you mean by that?'

'You and Max. If you're not an item now, you soon will be. I've seen the way he looks at you when you don't know it. I bet you're the only reason he's picked up a paint brush this week.'

Her heart gave a sudden thud. 'You're completely wrong about that. He's friendly and he likes talking about art, but it's no more than that.'

'And what's more, every instinct tells me that you fancy him like mad. You're as bad as he is, always watching him when he's not looking. Cupid's arrow has hit you, too.'

'Really, Nick. You've got it totally wrong, it's not like that at all.' She stared anxiously at him.

'Maybe, but I don't think so.' He stared morosely into his glass, and sighed. 'And I definitely haven't got it wrong about Clare really liking Stephen. I wish I could hate him for it, but I can't. He's a pretty cool guy.'

'But getting a girl this week would have been no more than a bonus, wouldn't it? It won't have been the reason that you came on the course, I'd be very surprised if it were. You weren't to know that you'd meet someone like Clare.'

He smiled at her. 'You're right. I

didn't come looking for love, so to speak.'

'So why *did* you decide to do the course, Nick? If you don't mind me saying so, you're not the sort of person I would have expected to choose to spend his holiday learning about watercolour.'

'I don't mind you saying so at all. In fact, it's a compliment.' He grinned at her. 'Sorry and all that, but it is. First of all, it's not my proper holiday — I'm going with my pals to Cyprus in August. This week's just an extra. I had some holiday to use up, saw the ad for the watercolour classes, and signed up on a whim.'

'Do you have a secret longing to be an artist, then?'

'It's even cornier than that. You know my surname's Williams. Well, my mother's nuts about the watercolours done by that Welsh chap, Kyffin Williams. No relation. Mum's going to be fifty soon, so I thought I'd do her a watercolour as a birthday present.'

'That's a really lovely idea, Nick. And have you enjoyed the week so far?'

'Funnily enough, I have enjoyed it on the whole. But I wouldn't go on another course like this again — it's not really me. By the end of the week, though, I'll have a present for Mum, and I'll have done something different. Yeah, I guess it's been all right.' The sound of approaching voices came from within the house. 'Don't tell anyone why I came on the course, will you?' he added quickly. 'I'd lose all credibility.'

'Of course, I won't. Rest assured, your terrible secret's safe with me,' she said, glancing towards the patio doors. 'We're about to be joined by the honeymoon couple, I suspect.'

'Now they're something else,' he said. 'I can't see how Howard can put up with that ghastly woman. I don't know about love being blind, but it's certainly deaf in his case.'

'Shush, Nick. Hello, you two.' She smiled up at Paula and Howard as they came up to the table.

Nick stood up. 'I'm on drinks duty this evening.'

'Oh, thank you, Nick. That's very sweet of you.' Paula sat down next to Jennifer. 'Wasn't it a simply lovely day today?'

'I'm glad that you enjoyed it.'

'We certainly did,' Howard remarked, and he strolled over to the display of watercolours and began to look at them.

A few minutes later, Nick returned with the drinks. He gave one to Paula, took the other over to Howard, and sat down again. 'So what did you get up to in Assisi, Paula? I didn't see you and Howard at all today.'

'We've been to Assisi once before,' Howard said, leaving the paintings and coming to sit next to Paula. He put his arm around her. 'We were only engaged the last time. We weren't there for long, but it was long enough to do all the touristy things, like see the Church of St. Francis. So today we did the not-so-touristy things.'

'Such as?' Nick asked.

'Mainly wandering through the narrow mediaeval streets at the top end of town. There aren't as many tourists up there. We photographed all the places we thought would make good watercolours, pottered around a bit, and finally ended up in the main *piazza* where we had coffee. Oh, and Paula bought one or two things.'

'I didn't realise you'd been to Umbria before,' Jennifer said in surprise. 'How long were you here?'

'Not long, just a week,' she said. 'We were on a whirlwind coach tour of the highlights of Tuscany and Umbria. For all it was short, it was an absolutely wonderful tour. We mentally marked it down as a place worth spending some time in. Then we saw the art course advertised and had to come.'

'It's certainly an unusual sort of honeymoon.' Nick said.

'We like being active, don't we, Howie?'

'Riveting stuff,' Nick muttered under

his breath. Jennifer sent him a warning frown.

'Are you flying back to England at the end of the week or are you going to go on somewhere else first?' Jennifer asked, turning back to Paula and Howard.

'We've got a flight booked for a week on Saturday,' Howard told her. 'We're going to hire a car for a week and drive from here to the area around Arezzo. When we come across interesting-looking places, we'll find an *agritourismo* and stay the night.'

'Which is why we're travelling light,' Paula explained. 'We've only got one suitcase between us so that we can easily move from place to place. Not that I need any more than that, not when I have my Howie with me. He's all I need.' She gazed adoringly at her husband.

'So that's why you were talking to the car-hire man, the one from the place next to the internet café!' Nick exclaimed.

Howard's hand slipped from Paula's shoulder. He straightened up. 'What are you talking about?'

'Clare saw you talking to him when we were in Montefalco last Sunday.'

Paula leaned closer to Howard and nestled up to him. 'Yes,' she trilled. 'But he charges too much. We're making other arrangements. That's one of the reasons why we'd like to use the internet.'

'How come you were able to understand the man?' Nick asked. 'I didn't think he spoke English.'

'Don't you believe it! Most of them do,' Howard said with a laugh, 'but some like to pretend that they don't. They get sick of tourists coming to Italy and expecting everyone to speak English, and I don't blame them to be honest. I know that Paula and I are among the worst offenders, but we're definitely going to make a start on learning Italian before we come again.' He looked towards the house. 'The others are taking their time. I

148

suppose we could . . . '

'Here we are!' Clare called gaily, appearing round the side of the house with Stephen at her side.

'Where did you come from?' Howard asked.

'Stephen wanted me to see Max's house.' Clare's face was wreathed in smiles. 'We had a cup of tea with Max on the *loggia*, and then Stephen and I went for a short walk around the garden. It's really lovely there.'

Howard and Paula exchanged glances.

'Your uncle said we could use the internet, Stephen,' Howard began. 'He said that at dinner the other evening.'

'And that we could take a peek at his paintings at the same time. Not the ones he did himself,' Paula giggled, 'but the ones he's got on his walls. Do you think we could pop across now?' She glanced at her watch. 'There's still plenty of time before dinner. We wouldn't be long.'

Stephen looked worried. 'Now's not really a very good time. When we went off for our walk, Uncle went to have a shower, and then he was going to come over and join us. I should think he'll be here pretty soon. Why don't you wait till he gets here, and then ask him if you can go across tomorrow?'

'What's this about tomorrow?' Max asked, coming up behind Stephen and Clare.

Nick's words about the way in which she and Max kept staring at each other jumped into Jennifer's mind. Her eyes involuntarily flew to Max's face, and she blushed.

'I didn't realise you were only just behind us,' Stephen told Max. 'You should have called to us and we would have waited for you.'

'You didn't exactly look as if you were anxious for company,' Max replied. He glanced at Stephen and Clare in amusement.

Howard half rose from his chair. 'I was asking Stephen about the internet, Max. Paula and I were wondering if we could check our e-mails tomorrow morning, and perhaps use the internet for a few minutes after that.'

'And maybe take a little peek at your paintings at the same time,' Paula added. She gave Max a coy smile.

'I don't see why not, providing that it fits in with the plans for tomorrow. What are tomorrow's plans, Jennifer?'

'I've moved the optional visit to the vineyard from tomorrow afternoon to Friday. We did a lot of travelling today and I thought we should have a rest tomorrow. The plan now is to stay here and put together the sketches and ideas we've been working on. Then we're going to talk about how we could use them as the basis for a larger, more ambitious project. As far as tomorrow evening goes, I've booked dinner at a restaurant in Montefalco. Carlo's going to drive us there.'

Max smiled. 'It sounds a perfect day.'

She beamed at him. 'Does that mean that you're joining us tomorrow?'

'It does indeed. By staying at home today, I've been able to catch up with everything urgent. I can now give myself a break tomorrow.' He turned to Howard. 'Why don't you and Paula come across straight after breakfast? Use the computer, and then have a look at the pictures. It won't take long. I'll come back with you, and we'll easily be here in time for the lesson.'

'That's so kind of you, Max.' Paula sighed.

'Paula's right, it's very sporting of you, Max. We both . . . ' Howard's words were drowned by a loud crash.

They all turned sharply. George was standing at the edge of the terrace, staring helplessly down at the two framed watercolours he'd knocked over.

'Oh, dear me,' he said. 'I do apologise — so very careless of me.' Stephen rushed forward and picked up the paintings. 'Thank you, dear boy. So kind. How clumsy of me.' He looked apologetically at them. 'I'm afraid that once again, I'm guilty of sleeping for too long.'

Jennifer got up, went over to him, put

her hand gently under his elbow and led him to the table. 'There's no such thing as sleeping too long, George. If you're tired, you need to rest. It's as simple as that. We walked a long way today.'

She helped him to his chair.

'How kind you are, Jennifer. Thank you.' He settled himself into his chair, and Nick put a drink on the table in front of him.

'Did you like what you saw of Assisi, George?' Max asked, pulling out a chair and sitting down next to him.

'I did indeed. It's a truly beautiful town. I must confess though, that the hills make it difficult for someone like me with old bones to get around. I did, however, manage the short walk down to the Basilica of San Francesco, steep though it was.'

'That's quite a walk,' Max said. 'Even on a cool day.'

'I was keen to look at the church's architecture, but there was a service about to start, so I decided not to go in until afterwards. Instead I sat in the sun and watched the world go by.'

'Ah, here's Maria. It looks as if our meal is on the way. I hope you've left some room for dinner, George. We'll need all our creative skills tomorrow, and a good meal tonight will help,' Jennifer said.

She included Max in the wide smile she gave the small group. He smiled back at her.

Nick's words sprang again to the fore of her mind, and she stood up.

\* \* \*

The meal finished and the group turned in for the night. Jennifer stared along the deserted table at Max, who showed no inclination to move.

'I'm not surprised that they've all turned in so early this evening,' she said, playing nervously with her empty glass. 'I think we're all pretty much worn out after our day in Assisi.'

'Well, if you're tired, you certainly

don't look it,' he said, and he got up and came and sat next to her. She inhaled the smell of him, the muskiness of his aftershave, the heat of his skin.

'I missed you today, Jennifer,' he said softly. 'All day long, I kept wondering what you were doing.'

Her heart missed a beat.

She knew that she should get up and go to bed.

On a balmy evening in a spotlit garden, the air filled with the heady fragrance of the fading day, the two of them alone beneath glittering stars and fairy lights that twinkled in the leaves above, it would be so easy to lose her focus, to forget the past and to give in to the present. Much too easy.

But she mustn't do that, she couldn't. Not even if she wanted to, and she didn't.

It was just that he was so close to her. His physical nearness was making her feel things that she didn't want to feel. It was making her wish that he'd encircle his arms around her and draw her close to his chest. But she shouldn't feel that way. Not with him. Not with the man who helped to destroy her father. She could never lose her heart to someone who'd done what he'd done. What would that make her?

And what sort of person must she be turning into if she could think about taking advantage of his feelings for her, knowing that he cared for her? But she had no choice — it was the reason she'd come to Italy. It was what she had to do.

But not that evening.

She'd do what she had to the following day. She'd need a clear mind for what she was trying to find out, and her mind was anything but clear at that moment.

He moved imperceptibly closer.

The air was stifling — she couldn't breathe.

She jumped up and stepped back from the table. 'Whatever I look like, I do feel tired. I'll see you tomorrow, Max.' She paused for a moment. 'I'm very much looking forward to it,' she added. She smiled into his eyes, then turned away fast.

But not so fast that she missed the look of pleasure that spread across his face.

# Suspicious Behaviour

Jennifer jumped out of her bed, went over to the window and threw open the shutters. The air was alive with the sound of birds singing and distant dogs barking. Sunshine spilled on to the stone floor of her room, bathing her in the bright morning light. She leaned forward, her elbows resting on the narrow window-sill, and stared at the view.

Framed by the window, lush green grass led up to a low wooden trellis, around which white-petalled roses curled. Beyond the trellis, the grass stretched away to the rim of the slope, a verdant green spattered with colour from the wild flowers that grew among its blades. The steep descent of the olive trees down the slope to the plain below was marked by their feathery tips which reached up to the clear blue sky.

It was a scene that she absolutely had to capture in watercolour before she left Umbria.

She turned round to face her room, leaned back against the window and stared around her in trepidation mixed with excitement. The previous day, she and Max had taken a step forward in their relationship — they'd moved from being merely an employer and employee who got on well, to being friends. Admittedly, it was a friendship with romantic undertones, which she hadn't sought and didn't want, but it had brought her closer to achieving her goal.

But how she was going to make the leap from friendly banter to a discussion about wrong-doing in the past, wrong-doing of a very personal nature, she had no idea. She'd have to hope that at some point when she and Max were alone, he'd say something that she could use to lead him back to the past.

At the same time, she'd have to be on her guard. She mustn't in any way encourage him romantically — that wouldn't be fair on him. And as for her . . .

She glanced across the room at the clock next to her bed, and promptly straightened up. It was much later than she'd thought. She was annoyed with herself — she'd wanted to have finished her breakfast before Paula and Howard appeared on the terrace, but it might be too late for that now.

The moment she'd lain back on the pillow the night before, it had hit her that, if she went to Max's with the Andersons the following morning, she might have a chance to look around whilst he was showing them his computer. She was amazed that she'd almost missed seeing that she could turn the situation to her advantage — it just showed how any emotional involvement with Max could make her lose her focus.

There'd almost certainly be some photos on display at his house, and these would give her an excuse to start a conversation about his family and their business, which could lead to an opportunity to introduce the subject of her father. It was definitely worth a try.

Her last thoughts before she'd fallen asleep were that she'd get up early, have breakfast on the terrace and wait there for the Andersons to arrive. She'd tell them that she was going to go with them as she, too, was curious to see his paintings. She was sure that they wouldn't notice if, once they were there, she drifted away and started looking at things on her own.

But she might be too late now; they could have already gone.

She hurried into her bathroom and showered at speed. Then she put on her sky blue halter neck sundress, brushed her hair and clipped it on top of her head with a tortoiseshell comb, slipped into silver low-heeled sandals, and rapidly made her way to the terrace.

There was no sign of Paula and Howard, so they were either still at

161

breakfast or they'd already gone across to Max's.

She hesitated next to the buffet table, not sure what to do. The place settings on the table were untouched, which suggested that no-one else had yet breakfasted, but the Andersons always ate alone, so that might not be true. She could always hang around for a while to see if they appeared, but if she did so, she'd run the risk of getting trapped in conversation with the next person to arrive, and she didn't want that. If they'd already gone to Max's, she needed to get there while they were still using the computer.

'*Buon giorno!*' Maria came on to the terrace with a pot of coffee and a jug of fresh milk. She put them on the table and turned to leave, but Jennifer called to her and asked if the Andersons had had their breakfast yet.

They'd asked to eat a little earlier that day, Maria told her. They'd finished eating and gone out. But it wasn't long ago, it couldn't have been more than a few minutes.

That helped her decision — it would take them some time to check their e-mails and find a car hire, let alone look at Max's paintings, so she'd have time to grab a bowl of cereal and a quick coffee.

She tipped some flakes into a bowl, added milk, picked up her spoon and went and sat down.

'Good morning, Jennifer. Or should I say *Buon giorno?*'

She groaned inwardly, and looked up. George was approaching the table, a wide smile on his face.

He took the place opposite her. 'What a glorious day this is, Jennifer. Painting in the garden is going to be most pleasant after our exertions of yesterday.'

'It is lovely, isn't it? Can I get you anything? Cereal maybe, or a piece of cake?'

'I think I shall have some cake this morning, but not until I've had my cup of tea. I find that I'm getting quite used to the Italian breakfast.'

'I suspect you're the only one. I still prefer cereal and I'm sure that the others do, too.'

A moment later, Maria came out with hot water and tea bags, which she put next to George. Jennifer started to eat her cereal quickly.

'You seem to be in a hurry, dear lady,' George observed.

'I am.' She finished the cereal, picked up her coffee and gulped it down. 'I'm afraid I'm going to have to ask you to excuse me now. I want to get over to Max's while the Andersons are still there, and I'm not sure how much longer they'll be. Like Paula, I'm keen to see his paintings, and it suddenly occurred to me that it would be less invasive to do so at the same time as they did.'

'How thoughtful, my dear. Nevertheless, I'm sure that he'd be delighted to show them to you at any time.'

She glanced across the table at him. His eyes were twinkling.

She looked at him suspiciously. 'What are you trying to say, George?'

'That I rather suspect that he'd prefer to show you his paintings when the two of you were by yourselves.'

'This is about the paintings and nothing else.'

'Of course it is. Why else would you want to visit the home of a delightful man, who clearly finds you quite delightful, too?'

She forced a laugh and stood up. 'You and Nick are as bad as each other, and you're both wrong. I won't be long — after all, it's only a small collection. You can make a start on your work when you've finished eating, if you want. Would you tell the others that, please?'

* * *

She hurried across the terrace and made her way up the side of the house to the path that ran between the cypress trees, linking their garden with Max's.

She half ran along the path, but slowed to a fast walk when she came out on the lawn in case anyone should be looking out of the windows.

Glancing to her left as she made her way across the grass, she was relieved to see that the wrought-iron gates at the top of the wide drive leading to both of the houses were still locked, a heavy padlocked chain was coiled around the two gates. At least Max was still in the house and hadn't gone off anywhere while Paula and Howard were sorting out their e-mails.

As she drew near to the *loggia*, she saw that the French windows at the back of the house were open. She'd go in that way rather than walk round to the front, she decided. She knew that that was what Stephen did for convenience and she was certain that Max wouldn't mind if she followed Stephen's example.

She reached the *loggia*, and stepped on to it between supporting stone pillars around which clusters of pink roses grew. At the same moment, the French windows flew open even wider and Stephen came bounding through them out of the house.

He glanced in her direction, and stopped short.

'Jennifer! What a surprise. I was just coming over to join you all. I decided to have breakfast with the others today. Do you know where you're going or do you want me to take you to Uncle?'

'I'm fine, thanks, Stephen. I thought I'd come across and check on Paula and Howard. They said they were going to try to hire a car for Saturday, and it occurred to me that they might need some help with the Italian,' she added with a flash of inspiration.

'They seem to be doing all right, as far as I can tell. Howard's on the internet and Paula's having a guided tour of the place. Well, if you're sure that you're OK and you don't mind going in on your own.'

'You get off, Stephen — you don't

want to keep Clare waiting.' She laughed. 'But thank you for the offer.'

'I'll see you later, then.' He grinned, gave her a little wave and started to run across to the cypress trees.

She went up to the French windows, hesitated a moment, and then went through them into the house. Pausing, she looked curiously around her at what was obviously a sitting room. Whoever had planned the interior design had managed the difficult feat of making the room look both comfortable and, at the same time, stylish.

Going a little further into the room, her gaze fell upon a huge oil painting hanging on the wall above the open fireplace. She stared up at it, mesmerised. The painting was a stunning blend of greens on a stone-coloured background, absolutely perfect for its position in the room, but a fascinating exercise in colour in itself.

With great difficulty, she tore her eyes away from the painting, telling herself that she was meant to be looking for photographs, not staring at wonderful pictures, and she continued looking around the room.

And she found what she wanted. There were three silver-framed photographs standing on a slender mahogany table next to the wall. She quickly went over to them. The first was of a very young Stephen. He was leaning against a dark-haired woman, who was laughing down at him. That must be his mother, she thought.

The other two were of the same man — Stephen's father, Peter. There was no mistaking the face that she'd first seen in the obituary. In the first of the photos Peter was by himself, staring into the camera. In the other, he had his arm around Max's shoulders and they were standing in front of what looked like a large warehouse. Max couldn't have been more than about fifteen or sixteen at the time.

That must be one of the family's warehouses, she decided, and she picked up the photo and peered at it.

'And in here you'll see the painting that I had commissioned in London earlier this year. It's by one of my favourite artists.' Max's voice came from just outside the sitting room door.

She stood rooted to the spot, unable to move, the photograph in her hand. The door opened and Max came into the room, closely followed by Paula.

'Just have a look at this, Paula, it's . . . Why, Jennifer!' he exclaimed. His face broke out into a broad smile of pleasure and he took a step towards her. 'What a lovely surprise.'

At the same moment, Paula turned sharply towards her. Anger flashed across Paula's face, and then it was gone and Paula was smiling brightly.

'You should have told us that you wanted to come across, too, Jennifer,' she said. 'We would have waited for you. Silly you.' She gave a little girl laugh.

Paula's bright smile didn't quite reach her eyes, she noticed.

Jennifer put the photograph back

down on the table.

'I'm sorry for barging in on you like this,' she said, moving over to them. 'It was a sudden afterthought. When I woke up I remembered that you were going to hire a car, Paula, and I thought you might like some help with the Italian.'

'We didn't have any problems, thank you. You can get an English translation online. So the language issue wasn't a problem, and we knew it wouldn't be. But thank you for the thought, anyway,' she added.

Turning her back on Jennifer, she started to look around the room, and then stopped. 'Oh, Max!' she exclaimed, pointing to the painting that hung above the fireplace. 'Is that the painting you said you'd had commissioned?' She moved over closer to it. 'It has such feeling to it, such movement.'

'That's the one. And that completes my collection, such as it is.'

She glanced at him over her shoulder. 'It's a wonderful collection. Truly it is,' she said tremulously. 'What a thrill to be surrounded by such beauty every day. Don't you think so, Jennifer?'

'Yes, I do.'

'But aren't you afraid that people might break in and steal the paintings?' Paula asked, frowning slightly. 'They must be worth a lot. I'd be so frightened that I wouldn't be able to sleep at night.'

'Not really. It's only a modest collection, and I don't make a point of going round telling people what my hobby is. The windows and gates are locked at night and whenever the house is empty, so the place is as safe as Fort Knox. The shutters lock automatically — you don't even have to remember to lock them yourself. No, I don't think anyone could get in, were they so minded.'

Paula turned back to the oil painting and stared up at it. 'I love all of your pictures, Max, and this one is particularly stunning, but it's my second favourite, not my favourite — my favourite is that darling still-life on the landing. I love the effect of the light on the fruit. Why don't you show it to Jennifer and see if she agrees with me that it's absolutely the most wonderful thing ever?'

'OK. Jennifer,' he said with a smile. 'Let's see if your definition of the most wonderful thing ever is the same as Paula's.'

'Whilst you're doing that, Max, I'll go and have a look at the view from the *loggia*. That's a picture in itself, albeit an ever-changing one.'

'That's fine, go right ahead. Come on, Jennifer. And we can see how Howard's getting on whilst we're up there.'

They heard the sound of Howard clattering down the stairs, two at a time, as they went out into the hall. Seeing them coming towards the stairs, he came to a stop on the bottom step.

'You'll find Paula on the *loggia*,' Max said with a smile. 'I hope you got everything done that was on your list.'

He made as if to go round Howard, but Howard stayed where he was, slightly blocking the staircase.

'I thought I heard your voice, Jennifer. I'm very grateful to you, Max. Yes, mission definitely accomplished. At least, I hope it is.'

'Where does the hope come in?'

'We asked to have the car brought here on Saturday morning, but it turns out that they've got an operative coming to the area today, he's got to pick up a car near here this evening and return it to them, and they asked if he could bring us our car tonight. They wouldn't charge us for the extra day. Apparently, it's cheaper for them if we take the car today than if we make them send out someone on Saturday who then has to be got back to their office.'

'I don't see what the difficulty is. Of course you must take the car today if that's what they want you to do.'

'Well, that's what I've provisionally said we'll do. But I wanted to check with you first that it was all right. I can change the arrangement if it isn't. The point is, we'd have to bring the car back here this evening so we'd need to have the gates open. We couldn't risk leaving a hired car outside on that narrow road all night.'

'That shouldn't be a problem. What time do you think you'll get the car?'

'I'm not quite sure. We thought we'd go up to Montefalco in the late afternoon, wait for the car, and then bring it back here. If you've already left for the restaurant by the time we get back, we'll dump the car and come up on foot and join you.'

'Well, why not stay in Montefalco if the driver's late getting there? You could go to the restaurant and meet us there. Then you could drive the car back after dinner.'

'I was going to do that, but then I realised that if I did, I wouldn't be able to have a drink. George has been going on and on about the bottle of wine he's going to treat us to this evening, and I'm very keen to try it. That's why I thought we'd leave the car at the house and walk back into town. It'd be a crying shame not to have a drink on our first and last restaurant dinner together.'

'What I suggest is, if you're not back by the time we have to set off, we'll leave the main gates closed, but unlocked. It's not as if it's going to be for very long. But you mustn't forget to padlock them when you leave,' Max said.

'We won't. I promise. Thanks a lot, Max.' He threw him a grateful smile. Stepping to the side of the stair, he stared over Jennifer's shoulder towards the sitting room. 'I suppose I'd better go and find Paula. It's time we made a start on our work. I can't wait to get started on a picture that'll have you reaching for your wallet, Max.'

All three laughed, and Howard left them and went in search of Paula.

'Let's have a coffee,' Max suggested.

'While that sounds very nice, I don't really think I should. I ought to follow the Andersons' example and get back to the class. I've already been here much longer than I intended.'

He grinned at her. 'I take it that's a yes, then. And so it should be, they'll be fine. You've taught them a huge amount in a week, and it's up to them now to put everything together as they think best. So, let's have that coffee.'

★ ★ ★

Sitting side by side at the large round table on the corner of the *loggia*, they stared across the garden to the shadowy outline of the distant hills, grey shapes veiled in the last traces of the morning mist.

'What a view.' Jennifer sighed. 'You've got beauty outside your house and beauty inside it, too. You've an excellent eye for aesthetics, Max. Your appreciation of line and colour can't be taught, it's something that you're either born with or you're not. You've made some wise investments.'

A look of pleasure swept across his face. 'I've never thought about it like that. Be careful! In a minute I'll be sacking you and taking over the classes myself,' he said with a laugh. 'But seriously, I don't even think about their worth. They're not for sale, they're for me to enjoy, not for me to make money from.' He paused, and glanced at her. 'Of course, collecting pictures, as with anything else, is much more fun when you can share your passion with someone else. Wouldn't you agree?'

His dark eyes remained on her face.

She picked up her cup, and put it down again.

She'd no idea why she suddenly felt as nervous as she did about the change in the direction of their conversation, about the caress in his tone of voice. After all, the closeness that was developing was what she'd hoped for when she'd come to Italy. She should feel triumphant, and be alert and ready to profit from the situation. She shouldn't be feeling lost and confused. But she was.

'Don't you agree, Jennifer?' he repeated quietly.

Struggling to make sense of her emotional turmoil, she took one of the *amaretti* from a ceramic dish in the centre of the table and started to unwrap it.

'Of course, I do,' she said, directing her attention to the paper that had been round the biscuit. 'Everything is much better when you can talk about it with a friend.'

He sat back in his chair, and stared hard at her. 'I'm curious about something. Tell me, why did you come here this morning? Don't get me wrong, I'm delighted that you did. But why *did* you come?'

She stopped playing with the paper and looked at him, startled. 'I told you, I wanted to help the Andersons with any Italian they needed.'

'Now why don't I believe you? Could it be that my disbelief is caused by my certainty that you know as well as I do that you don't need to speak Italian to hire a car online in Italy? Could that be why I suspect you came over for a totally different reason?' He leaned forward. 'Or do I just want to think that it was?'

She blushed. 'Believe it or not, it's the truth.'

He straightened up and smiled wryly at her. 'And that's why you were looking at the photos of my family when I came upon you, is it? Despite the urgency of your desire to help the Andersons, you left them to struggle on without you while you stopped to look at my photos.'

'I was just curious.'

'About what?'

This was it! This was the moment she'd been waiting for, and she had to give it everything she could.

'About what your family looked like. And about you.' She glanced up at him from under her eyelashes. 'I haven't met many businessmen before, but I can't believe that there are many like you, with business prowess, a passion for art and real taste. I suppose I wanted to know more about you, and your family seemed the right place to start.'

She let her clear blue eyes linger on his face.

He reached out, took her hand and stroked it gently with his index finger. Her insides dissolved into liquid honey. 'That's what I hoped you'd say because I feel the same about you, Jennifer. You must have sensed that. I want to know everything that there is to know about you, your family, the things that made you the lovely person you are.'

She pulled her hand away. His gentle caress was affecting her too much. It was stopping her from thinking clearly, making her want to give in to the way she was feeling — the way she couldn't stop herself from feeling, hard though she tried. And that could never be.

'And I feel the same way, too, Max' she said, her voice hoarse to her ears. 'But I know that I shouldn't, you're the man I work for and I mustn't let myself forget that, much as I might want to.' She put her hands up to her flushed cheeks, stood up and pushed back her chair. 'I really must get back to the class now. They'll have started on their projects a while ago and I ought to see how they're doing.' She took a step away from the table, and paused. 'I'm sorry, I've no choice.'

'I'll see you at lunch, then. I'm going to do my drawing project here. There's a wonderful view from my bedroom window. I'm going to include the window-frame, too. It'll be a sort of frame within a frame.'

'How funny!' she exclaimed, dropping her hands. 'I was also going to paint the view from my window, including the frame.'

His face broke into a smile of triumph. He stood up and went round the table to her. 'You see, Jennifer, we're kindred spirits, just as I thought. And kindred spirits definitely trumps boss and employee.'

Her knees trembled. She couldn't move.

'Yes,' he said, raising his hand and gently pushing her hair back from her face. 'Kindred spirits.'

She looked up into eyes that were flecked with gold, eyes that were gazing down at her with love. Her power of movement returned, and she spun round and ran towards the cypress trees.

# The Deception Is Revealed

Stephen sighed deeply and rubbed his stomach. 'Do we really have to wait for Howard and Paula to get here, Jennifer? I'm starving.'

She glanced at her watch. 'I must say, I thought they'd be here by now.'

'They've probably changed their mind about coming.' Nick's voice was tinged with irritation. 'The two lovebirds want to be on their own.'

Stephen and Clare glanced at each other and giggled.

'I rather doubt that, Nick,' Jennifer said with a smile. She turned to Max, who was sitting next to her. 'Do you think we should order now, Max? I rather think they'd have got here by now if they were intending to join us.'

George shifted to a more comfortable position in his chair. 'If I may say so, I agree with you, Jennifer. And like

Stephen — I certainly feel ready to eat.'

'I'm quite hungry, too,' Clare said.

Jennifer picked up her menu. 'That decides it then. We'll order now and if the Andersons turn up later on they can order for themselves. I don't know why on earth they didn't stay in Montefalco once they'd collected the car. It would have been so much more sensible.'

George gave a sudden exclamation. 'How slow of me! I've just realised that I might be able to benefit from Howard having a car.' He beamed across the table at Jennifer. 'You'll recall that I told you I was returning to the vintner tomorrow, Jennifer? I arranged it last Sunday. He's going to bring in a superior Sagrantino wine for me to taste, one that will be considerably better than anything we have this evening.'

She heard Nick snigger. Under the table, she kicked Nick's foot. 'Yes, I do remember,' she said.

'I'd been wondering how to get up here. The steep climb wouldn't be a problem for you young things, but it'd be a challenge for my old limbs, and I didn't really want to ask if Carlo if he would bring me up in the minibus since this is a personal visit . . . '

'Oh, but you should,' Jennifer cut in. 'He's there to help.'

'That's very kind, dear lady. But Howard having a car solves the problem, and I won't need to trespass upon Carlo's time. I can't imagine that Howard would mind running me up to the *piazza* at some point. I can make my own way back. Going downhill is quite a different matter.'

'That's an excellent idea, George. I'm sure that Howard would be delighted to help out. And you might not be the only person who wants to come up to the town tomorrow, it's always possible that someone will find that they need to buy some last-minute things. Ah, here comes the waiter with more bread and olives. Right, if we're all ready, we'll order now.'

She ordered *antipasto* for the table.

Then they each gave the waiter their order for the main course and he left.

Jennifer looked around the table. 'It's a real shame that we aren't all here. It's the only dinner that we have out in the week.'

'I'm surprised that you didn't pick tomorrow night for the final beanfeast, Friday being the last night and all,' Nick remarked.

'I was going to at first, but in the end I changed my mind.'

'How come? Going out on tomorrow would have brought the week to a rousing finale, I would have thought.'

'That's true. But in the end, I thought it better to leave tomorrow evening clear for any last-minute packing. Also, you might want an early night before you embark on a day with a lot of travelling. Not to mention that there'd be less risk of you having to travel with a hangover.'

They all laughed.

'You've got a point there.' Nick grinned at George.

'You can take it really easily tomorrow. Paint, relax by the pool, read, whatever you like. If you want, you can visit a local vineyard in the afternoon. Though I'd be careful how much tasting I did, if I were you. Especially you, George, if you have the Sagrantino ahead of you.'

'You can be sure that I'd exercise moderation,' George remarked.

'I'll need to confirm the time all of you have to leave for the airport on Saturday,' she went on. 'But if I remember rightly, everyone's leaving quite early, in which case it'd probably be wise to do most of the packing tomorrow. Apart from Paula and Howard, that is. They can take their time as they don't have a flight to catch.'

'You needn't worry about their packing. It's done. Or rather not undone,' Clare said.

Jennifer laughed. 'That sounds convoluted. What do you mean, Clare?'

'Paula's already packed one of her cases.'

'How come you know that?' Nick asked.

'Idiot.' Clare pretended to throw a piece of bread at him. 'No, I saw an open suitcase when I was passing their room this morning, didn't I? It was full to the brim and Paula was kneeling next to it. I made a comment about her being on the ball with her packing, and she said that they hadn't used the things in that case. She'd only opened it to get some more toothpaste or something like that. They'd used the clothes in their other suitcase as a way of making sure that they'd have a case of clean clothes for the second week.'

'Aha! Here comes our *antipasto*,' George said, as the waiter appeared carrying two large round wooden boards. He picked up his napkin and tucked it into the neck of his shirt while the waiter was placing the boards in the centre of the table, followed by a basket of fresh bread between the platters.

'Ooh, look at that!' said Clare, gazing at the food in front of them.

'Yes, that does look quite delicious,' George murmured. He leaned forward, his eyes shining as he gazed at the variety of cold cuts, cheeses and grilled vegetables on the board closest to him. He glanced across to the second board, which was filled with a variety of *crostini* and *bruschette*. 'Yes, quite delicious,' he repeated. 'If it weren't a cliché, I'd say that it all looks good enough to eat.'

He smiled around the table in satisfaction.

'Good enough to eat and good enough to paint,' Nick added. 'But preferably not in that order.'

Jennifer sat very still, staring at the table with unseeing eyes. Something was niggling away in the back of her mind and she couldn't quite put her finger on it.

One of them had made a comment a few minutes earlier that had jarred, but it had slipped into the back of her mind, just out of reach, and she couldn't get hold of it. If only she could bring it forward and see what it was. It was something that had struck her as strange when it had been said.

'Come on, Jennifer. There soon won't be anything left,' Max said, his eyes warm upon her face.

'This *prosciutto* is really yummy,' Clare said, happily. 'But I've got a horrible feeling that I've taken a bit too much. If I eat everything on my plate, I'll never have room for my *spaghetti*.'

Stephen put his arm round her shoulder. 'It's a case of your eyes being bigger than your stomach.' He pulled her gently to him and kissed the tip of her nose. 'And what lovely eyes they are. I could drown in them.'

'Yuck!' Nick rolled his eyes in mock disgust.

'That's it!' Jennifer cried out. 'They've only got one suitcase!'

They all stared at her in surprise.

'I'm afraid I don't follow you, dear lady,' George said.

'Who's only got one suitcase?' Max asked.

'They have — the Andersons. Don't you remember, Nick? You and I were talking yesterday evening while we were waiting for everyone else to arrive, and then Paula and Howard joined us. You were there, but not Clare and Stephen, and nor was George. I asked the Andersons where they were going on Saturday, if they were flying back to England like the rest of you, and they said that they had another week in Italy. They were going to drive around for a week and stay overnight in places they liked the look of.'

'I remember that,' Nick said. 'But what about it?'

'Paula said that they'd only brought one suitcase between them. They were sharing the suitcase. Travelling light would make it easier for overnight stops, she said.'

Nick stared at her. 'Well, yes, she did say something of the sort. I wouldn't swear to the details, though. But why does it matter?'

'It probably doesn't. It's just that it's

funny, in the light of what she said to Clare this morning about having a second suitcase. If they do have only one case, it means that they'd already packed it this morning, even though there are still almost two more days to go. That's peculiar, don't you think?'

'When she said that yesterday, she must have meant that they were using only one of their suitcases this week,' Max suggested, 'and saving the other for next week, which is what she told Clare. She probably phrased it badly.'

'I don't think she did mean that, that's not really travelling light, is it?'

'So you think she was deliberately lying?' he asked, frowning.

She shook her head. 'No, she can't have been. There'd be no reason to lie about such a thing. There must be a simple explanation.'

'I think she *was* lying,' Clare blurted out. 'She lied about speaking Italian, so why not lie about other things? Whatever you said, Nick, about the hire-car man probably being able to speak English, I know he was talking to them in Italian, it's the body language, and I know that the Andersons understood him. I've tried to kid myself that I was mistaken, but I wasn't.'

George wiped his mouth with his napkin. 'But, dear girl, why would Paula and Howard lie about speaking Italian? There's no reason to do so, is there, Jennifer?'

Max put down his knife and fork. 'Actually, there is,' he said slowly, 'if you don't want anyone to know that you're familiar with an area and may have friends and contacts there. I'm now thinking back to how keen Paula was to see my paintings, so keen that she virtually bulldozed me into showing her around . . . '

'And she asked you about your security.' Jennifer's words fell out on a rush. 'You told her about the shutter locks, and just after that, she was in the sitting room by herself for quite a while when we went to look at that still-life painting. At her suggestion. She could have easily disabled the most important locks in the time that she had. Oh, Max!' Her hands flew to her mouth.

'What's more, Howard kept us standing in the hall for ages while he talked about the hired car, which was something he could have done later on,' he added. 'And he was alone upstairs for some time, too.'

The blood drained from Jennifer's face. 'I know it's virtually impossible to believe, but could they be art thieves?'

'It's certainly beginning to look that way, and I'm not going to take any chances,' Max said grimly. He stood up, took his mobile phone from his pocket and held it out to her. 'The number for the police is one, one, two. Will you ring them, explain the situation and ask them to get to the house as fast as they can? Road blocks might be an idea, too.'

She took the phone from him. 'What are you going to do?'

'I'm going across the square to get Carlo,' he said. He glanced at the worried faces around the table. 'There's nothing the rest of you can do, so you might as well stay here and finish your meal.' He pulled out his wallet, took a handful of notes from it and handed them to Stephen. 'I'll leave you in charge of settling up, Stephen.'

He turned to Jennifer. 'Except for you, Jennifer. I hate to ask you to go anywhere where there might be trouble, but would you come back to the house with me? You'll stay outside in the minibus, of course and I'll lock it when I get out, but you'll be able to help with the police when they arrive. I don't know whether they speak English or not.'

'Of course, I'll come with you,' she said, tapping the number into the phone. 'But I doubt if we'll catch them. They'll be long gone by now.'

'Not necessarily,' Max said. 'We left the house later than we'd planned. They'll have allowed for that possibility, and they won't have dared to make a move until they were absolutely certain that we were out of the way and that it was well past the time that anyone would come back for something they'd forgotten. And once they're at the house, it'll take some time to get the paintings down and stack them in the car without damaging them. Remember, too, there are two houses to do.'

'*Polizia*,' she said into the phone.

'Come to think of it, they did seem very interested in the paintings in our house,' George said.

Stephen leapt to his feet. 'I'm coming, too. No way are you going on your own, Uncle. Here, Clare, you take the money.'

'I guess I can also do the heroic thing.' Nick got up. 'Count me in.'

'Thanks, boys; I appreciate it. I'll see you outside, Jennifer.' Max hurried out, closely followed by Stephen and Nick.

She rapidly explained the situation to the police, gave them the location and told them that they were going back to the house. Then she switched off the phone and bent down to pick up her bag.

As she did so, George pulled his napkin from his shirt and started to stand up.

She saw what he was doing and moved swiftly to his side. 'I know what you're thinking, George, but no.' She laid her hand on his arm. 'I'd be really grateful if you stayed here with Clare. I don't want her left on her own, and I definitely don't want her coming with us.'

'But I'm a nurse,' Clare insisted. 'You might need me.'

Jennifer tried to laugh. 'I'm sure it won't come to that.' Catching Clare's eye, she inclined her head towards George. Clare sat back, nodding that she'd understood.

# An Eventful Evening

Carlo swung the minibus off the main road and on to the narrow road leading to Max's house. He dimmed the headlights and slowed his speed, reducing the sound of the engine.

From her seat behind Max and Carlo, Jennifer kept her eyes fixed on the windscreen, her heart beating fast as she waited to see the wrought-iron gates that marked the top of the drive.

As her eyes gradually became accustomed to the gloom, she saw that the black mass was broken into fragments by the dots of bright light that came from the numerous houses spread out across the plain. At the heart of the valley, encircled by subtly spotlit walls, the ancient town of Bevagna shimmered beneath a halo of gold.

She glanced down the slope at the side of the bus and her heart gave a sudden leap. A line of shining stars was winding sinuously in their direction. She pressed closer to the window, her breath misting the glass — and yes, the starry lights were definitely coming towards them.

She sat back in her seat, weak with relief. 'I think I can see the police,' she said, her voice shaking. 'But they're still quite far away. We'd better stop now or we'll get to the house before the police do.'

Max gestured to Carlo to pull into the side, shut down the engine and turn off the lights. The minibus rolled a little way forward and came to a standstill just before the road curved sharply to the left.

Stephen leaned in front of Jennifer and stared down at the moving lights. 'You're right, Jennifer. It must be the police.'

Max turned to look at Stephen, Nick and Jennifer, his face grim. 'Now listen to me carefully. I don't want any heroics tonight. I'm more than grateful that you want to help, but no-one, and that includes me, must take any chances. Pictures are only objects, and objects are nowhere near as important as people.'

'But there's no need for you to do anything, is there?' Jennifer asked, her heart in mouth. 'You might get hurt. The police can do what has to be done, can't they? They'll be here any moment now.'

'Distances are deceptive, especially at night, and I'm not sure how long they'll be. I need to see what's going on so I'm going to go on foot from here.' Stephen made a movement. 'By myself, Stephen. I want to see whether or not they're still there. If they are, there's less chance of me being seen if I'm alone.'

'Oh, Max. You'll be really careful, won't you? Promise me?' Her face white with fear, Jennifer reached out her arm to him. He leaned back and took her hand.

'I'll be very careful, I promise,' he said, his eyes on her face. 'I'm not your hero type. Don't you worry. I'll be back in no time.'

Giving her a reassuring smile, he squeezed her hand, then dropped it, slid open the door and got down from the minibus. 'No-one goes anywhere,' he called up, and he ran softly to the bend in the track and disappeared round it.

After what felt like an eternity, he came running out of the darkness. There was a collective sigh of relief the moment that they saw him.

'They're still there,' he told them in a low voice as he climbed back in. 'The gates are wide open, and the chain and padlock are hanging from one of the gates. There seems to be three of them — the Andersons and a man I didn't recognise.'

'I bet that's the man Clare saw them with,' Stephen said. 'What are they doing?'

'They were putting one of the paintings into the back of a light-coloured van. From the size of the picture I think it's the oil from the sitting room, which suggests that they're almost finished.'

'So it's a hired van, not a car!' Nick exclaimed. 'I bet you're right about the man, Stephen. And what's more, it'll be the grey van we saw in Montefalco.'

'The lights are on in both buildings, which means that they've emptied both houses. I imagine that they did the other house first as the van's now parked on the grass at the end of the drive, very close to the *loggia*. I think they're using the French windows, not the front door, which makes sense as it gives them more room to manoeuvre. You stay put, I'm going to have another look.'

'Don't go, Max! Wait for the police. They must almost be here by now.' Biting her nail, Jennifer peered out of the window down the slope. 'I can't see the lights any more so they must be on the hill behind us, and probably close to us.'

'Don't worry, Jennifer. I'll be fine. I'll

be back in a minute,' he said, and he jumped down and sped into the dark.

Moments later, he was climbing up the steps into the minibus again. 'I was right. They're very close to leaving. It looks as if Howard's about to shut the van doors.'

Nick slid to the edge of his seat. 'Then I say we go in and stop them. Apart from Jennifer, of course.'

'Wait!' Max ordered. 'That's not an option — they might have a gun.'

Stephen laughed dismissively. 'Not Paula and Howard.'

'Yes, Paula and Howard. This has been very carefully planned. No way are they innocent honeymooners, acting on the spur of the moment. It takes nerve to do what they're doing, not to mention skill and some knowledge of the art world. They'll need to have buyers for the pictures, for example. I'm certain this won't be their first theft and they'll know that Italian police are armed, which means that there's a real risk of them having a gun. No-one is charging in, but I've got an idea that could buy us some time. If it works, that is. We'll need to move sharpish, though.'

Jennifer twisted round and stared through the rear window. 'I'm sure I can hear police cars. We can leave it to them.'

'I'm not going to risk them getting away before the police get here, especially as I think I can safely stop them. Or at least slow down their exit.' Max tapped Carlo on the shoulder and gestured for him to follow him. Stephen started to rise from his seat. 'No, Stephen,' he said quickly. 'You and Nick stay here.'

Jennifer put her hand to her throat. 'Please, be careful, Max. Remember what you said about playing it safe. If they see you and they've got a gun . . . ' her voice trailed away. Panic welled up inside her.

'Rest assured, I won't do anything silly.' He gave her a quick smile, and he and Carlo got down from the minibus and ran towards the bend in the road.

Nick moved into the front seat. 'I'm going to ignore what Max said. They might need help.'

Stephen made a move to follow him, took one look at Jennifer's terrified face and sat back down again. He squeezed her arm reassuringly. 'They'll be fine, Jennifer. They're not stupid. And you're right about the police being close. I can hear them now. Nick and Uncle Max will be back in a minute, you'll see.'

He fell silent. Side by side, they stared into the darkness beyond the windscreen, waiting.

Almost as soon as he'd gone, Nick was back outside the minibus, standing at the foot of the steps.

'Max and Carlo have closed the gates,' he gleefully called up to them. 'Max wrapped the chain around the gates and put the padlock on. The goons in the van were too busy reversing up the slope to notice what was happening. Great stuff. I'm going to . . . '

He stopped short at the sound of

steps running towards them and clambered quickly into the van.

Panting, Max and Carlo climbed into the minibus, slammed the doors shut and threw themselves into their seats. Carlo revved the engine, thrust the gear into reverse and guided the minibus swiftly backwards, steering it close to the side of the mountain.

Behind them, the distant drone of approaching cars grew into a loud roar. Carlo braked hard.

Max turned to face the seats behind him. 'I'm sure Nick's told you what we've done — we saw you there, Nick. We've stopped them from driving out. The main thing now is to make sure that the police can get past us to the house. We don't want to block their way.'

'Do you think that Howard and Paula will ram the gates?' Nick asked.

'They might try, but they won't succeed. The chain's very strong. No, they're more likely to try to shoot the lock open.'

'Suppose they drive down the slope and escape that way.' Stephen stared anxiously at Max.

'A van like that couldn't stay upright on such a steep slope — they'd know that and they'd never risk it. Besides, there are trees all the way down the slope. They wouldn't have a prayer of a chance.'

'Suppose they come after us with a gun.' Jennifer's voice shook.

'They can't get through the gates any more than the van can. What they might do is ditch the van and go down the slope on foot, but it wouldn't be easy in the dark. And if they did that, they'd be going away from us.'

A car screeched to a halt behind them, and another behind that. The back of the minibus was suddenly flooded with light.

They turned to look through the rear window and saw two policeman step out of the first car that was parked behind them. One of them started to walk towards them, and the other waited by the side of the car.

One behind the other three more cars edged past the policemen and the minibus, and continued to the house.

'I forgot, the gates are locked!' Max exclaimed. 'They'll need the key for the padlock.' He jumped down from the minibus. 'Will you tell them where I'm going, Jennifer?' he called up.

'Of course, I will.' She moved forward and climbed out after him. Her heart pounded with fear as she saw him disappear round the corner. Then she turned to the policeman.

Standing in front of the wrought-iron gates, which were wide open, Jennifer watched Carlo drive off in the minibus, first of all to tell Maria what had happened and then to collect George and Clare from the restaurant.

When he was out of sight, she turned and started to walk down the drive and past the van which had been abandoned by the thieves in the middle of the drive. Seeing that the back doors of the van were open, she paused and glanced inside. There were several large crates, into each of which a number of paintings had been slotted. The oil painting from above the fireplace lay on top of one of the crates, half covered by a rug.

Two men in protective clothing were dusting the inside of the van for fingerprints, while a policeman stood by, watching them. She went over to the policeman and thanked him for their quick response to the call and for sending out so many men and cars. Their support had been amazing, she said.

There'd recently been a spate of robberies in the area, he told her, especially art-related robberies and they were very keen to catch the perpetrators. As soon as she'd phoned them and told them of her fears about a possible theft, they'd seen a chance to catch the criminals red-handed and had thrown everything they had behind it.

They'd also set up two road blocks,

he added, one just before the divide in the Bevagna road and the other at the entrance to Montefalco.

She thanked him again, and continued making her way down to Max, who was at the bottom of the drive, staring towards the end of the garden which was flooded with bright light thrown out by giant lamps. Stephen and Nick had gone across the grass and were standing as close to the top of the slope as the police would let them go, two black figures, stark against the white light.

She told Max what the policeman had said.

He looked down at her, and took her hand. 'It's just a matter of waiting, then. They won't be able to get far. It'll all soon be over.'

As he finished speaking, they saw two figures come up over the top of the slope and into the beam of one of the lamps. Stephen and Nick gave a shout of triumph and jumped up and down on the spot. Max's hand tightened around hers. 'And here's the first of them.'

'It's Howard!' she exclaimed.

The pair came nearer, and they saw that Howard's hands were behind his back. The slim policeman walking at his side was beaming with pride. Howard's face was an angry scowl.

Jennifer heard a nearby policemen say something to his colleague.

'Apparently that policeman's a champion runner,' she relayed to Max. 'We're very lucky that he was on duty tonight. Anyone racing against him didn't stand a chance.'

They watched Howard as he was led past them, his eyes firmly fixed on the ground. Turning slightly to look back at him they saw that he was in handcuffs. As they neared the cars the slim police officer said something to Howard and propelled him towards the nearest police car, indicating that he should get into the back seat.

Max dropped Jennifer's hand. 'It's no good. I'd really like a quick word with

Howard. Will you ask the officer if I can speak to him? I only want a minute.'

Jennifer ran up to the police officer and put Max's request to him. He glanced across, at Max then back to Jennifer, and nodded. Pulling Howard away from the car he gestured for Max to come over.

Max walked straight up to Howard who turned towards him, his face impassive.

'Why, Howard?' he asked quietly, coming to a stop in front of him. 'Why did you do it?'

The corner of Howard's mouth twisted into a sneer. 'I would have thought that the answer's fairly obvious. Redistribution of wealth, of course. From someone who's got money enough to waste large sums on expensive ornaments, to someone who needs enough money to buy the necessities of life. It's not that difficult to fathom it out if you look beyond your privileged world.'

'I've worked very hard for everything

I've got. As for you, you're trying to live off the fruit of my labour, and the labour of others, by the sound of it. If you genuinely needed money and couldn't earn it like everyone else, you could have tried asking for help.'

'What, go cap in hand to you and your ilk, begging for a handout? Ask you to throw us some crumbs out of the goodness of your hearts?' His voice rose and he laughed in derision. 'I don't think so. It's a bit beneath me and my wife. Just a bit.'

'And you don't think theft is beneath you?' Max said, contempt in his voice.

'Are you and Paula really on your honeymoon?' Jennifer asked, coming to stand next to Max.

Howard laughed even more loudly. 'You're even more gullible than I thought, Jennifer. Now, if there's nothing else . . . '

He shrugged the policeman's hand off his shoulder, turned and got back into the car.

A noise came from behind them and

they heard footsteps approaching. Jennifer turned to see what was going on. 'Look, they've got Paula, too!' she cried gleefully as she saw Paula being brought up the drive, a policeman on either side of her. One of them had a gun in his hand. 'She and Howard must have made a run for it together. Thank goodness neither got away. Even if the other man did.'

Paula drew alongside them. She glanced quickly towards the car that Howard was in and her steps slowed. He looked up at her through the window, and a rueful smile crossed his lips. She stopped and turned abruptly to Max and Jennifer.

'You pigs,' she hissed, and she threw them a look of pure hatred. 'You filthy pigs.'

One of the officers gave her a push to move her on. Her head held high, she walked forward and let herself be led towards a car that was parked further up the drive.

'Not travelling with Howie darling,

then?' Nick called after her as he and Stephen came running up to stand alongside Max and Jennifer.

A loud shout came from the bottom of the garden, followed by the sound of dogs barking in excitement. They spun round and stared at the top of the slope. Two policemen were giving the thumbs-up sign to their colleagues on the drive.

'That must mean that they've got the third man,' Max said. 'There's no hiding from dogs.'

A moment later, the head of the third thief appeared above the top of the slope, followed by the rest of his body. As he was led across the grass by a policeman on either side, they saw that the bottoms of his trousers were bloodstained and torn.

Jennifer turned to Max. 'It looks as if the dogs got him. He's lucky he wasn't seriously hurt. So now that they've caught the three of them, it's really over, Max, isn't it? I don't think I've ever been so scared in all my life.'

Her voice broke.

'My darling Jennifer. Yes, it is.' He put his arms around her and pulled her to him.

Encircled by his strong arms, she felt the warmth of his body spread through hers. The fears of the evening faded away, and she slid her hands around his back and nestled more closely to him. His arms tightened around her and his male scent enveloped her. Beneath his linen shirt, his chest was hard against her face. She clung to him more fiercely, and all sense of time and place dissolved into nothingness.

'Oh, Jennifer,' she heard him murmur into her hair, and she sank deeper into his embrace.

'*Signore*.' A policeman appeared at Max's side. '*Vorrebbe andare in casa con me?*'

'Oh, no, he wants you to go into the house with him,' Jennifer translated, her voice muffled by his shirt.

Max sighed, and let his arms fall to his side. Her heart racing, she stepped back from him, and for a long moment they stared into each other's eyes.

'*Signore*,' the policeman prompted.

'I suppose I'd better go in and start answering questions,' he said. 'What timing.'

'I'm coming with you,' she said, and she moved to his side, tucked her arm into his, and they followed the officer into the house.

# Quiet Reflection

Breakfast had been a quiet, sombre meal that morning. Once they'd finished eating, they'd been interviewed in turn by the police, with Jennifer translating each time. While the interviews were underway other officers had searched the Andersons' room and had bagged up the few things they'd left behind. Jennifer gave them the paintings they'd done and those had been taken away, too.

By the end of the morning they'd all felt completely drained, and lunch on the terrace had been as subdued as the breakfast. From the comments she'd heard the police make one to another, she knew that another group was working in Max's house, and that he'd had to stay over there with them so she wasn't surprised when he didn't turn up to have lunch with them.

'Come on, Clare,' Stephen said briskly when he finished his *panini*. He pushed away his empty plate and stood up. 'I'm not going to let your last full day in Umbria be ruined by the Andersons. We'll go into Montefalco and have our coffee there, and then we'll have a look around. And we can plan our first meeting in England, which can't come soon enough for me.' He glanced anxiously at Jennifer. 'It's OK to disappear now, isn't it, Jennifer? I'll go stir crazy if I don't get out for a bit. Clare, too.'

'Of course. You go and make the most of Clare's last day. She hasn't had much fun so far today — none of you have.'

'Are you sure that you don't mind us trotting off and leaving you with the police and everything?' Clare asked hesitantly.

'Of course I don't.' Jennifer smiled warmly at her. 'Nothing would give me greater pleasure than to see you enjoying yourselves.'

'Thanks.' Clare and Stephen went off, hand in hand.

George rose awkwardly to his feet. 'I find that I am somewhat tired, dear lady. I think I shall go to my room and have a short lie down. The events of yesterday and today have rather taken it out of me, not that that's anyone's fault but Howard and Paula's, mind you — but a moment or two to recoup is in order, I feel.'

'That sounds an excellent idea, George. We'll see you later.'

He nodded to Nick, gave a little bow to Jennifer and made his way slowly into the house.

'Right, one of us ought to do some work. I'm going to finish the picture for my mother,' Nick said. 'There's not a lot left to do, and I was tempted to leave the rest till I got home, but I know I'd never finish it if I did, and an unfinished picture wouldn't be much of a present for Mother Dearest.' He got up. 'I won't apologise for leaving you alone because I strongly suspect that you'll be delighted to have an afternoon without any of us around. I know that I would, if I were you.'

He gave her a knowing grin, crossed over to his paints and easel, gathered everything, together and went off into the garden, whistling.

She sank back into her chair. Nick was right, it was going to be much easier not to have to worry about them that afternoon. George wasn't the only one who was worn out — she felt absolutely shattered. The events of the night, and the words, 'My darling Jennifer', had gone round and round in her head, and she'd only slept fitfully. To have a relaxing afternoon by herself was an unexpected treat.

She sat back. She wasn't going to let herself think about Max, she wasn't going to let herself think about anything at all, there'd be plenty of time for that later. Resting her head on the back of the chair, she stared up at the lilac wisteria that was clinging to the grey stone walls of the house. Slowly, her eyes began to close.

'Where is everyone?' Max asked, coming round the comer of the house.

Her eyes flew open and she sat up sharply.

He took the seat opposite her. She saw that his face looked strained and drawn.

'I didn't expect to see you until much later,' she said, pushing her hair back from her face. 'I thought you'd be tied up with the police for longer.'

'They've been there all morning, taking fingerprints and the like. The insurance people are also there, I had to notify them about what happened. But fortunately they can manage without me now, so I decided to come and see you. I didn't expect to find you by yourself, though.'

'Stephen and Clare are in Montefalco, Nick's in the garden painting, and George is having a rest. Everyone's still very unsettled, but we're doing our best to get back to normal.'

'I'm not surprised, it's bound to take

a while to get over a shock like that.'

'What's the state of affairs here with the police?'

'They've taken down all of our statements, and they said that they've almost finished here. What about you? When they've done everything they have to do in your house, will you have to go the station with them? If so, I'll obviously come with you.'

'I don't think so. They've got my statement, and I've given them Howard and Paula's completed application forms. What a fiction those forms were! I can't think what else they'd need from me. I expect we'll both have to attend the trial, though, and possibly the others, too. If so, I'll pay everyone's expenses. I'm going to refund the cost of the week to them all, anyway. It's the least I can do.'

'That's very kind of you, seeing that it wasn't your fault in any way.'

'That may be. It's a sort of thank-you for their support yesterday.' He leaned slightly across the table towards her. At the look in his eyes, her heart gave a sudden lurch. 'And you, Jennifer,' he said, his voice warm. 'You were tremendous. I can't thank you enough.'

She gave an awkward laugh and wound a stray strand of hair behind her ear. 'Like everyone else, I was glad to do what I could to help.'

He straightened up. 'I want you to know it was much appreciated. I've given Maria the rest of the day off and I've booked a restaurant in Bevagna. I thought we'd have an early meal and then everyone can get a good night's sleep. Last night's meal was shot to pieces, and I want them to have an evening to remember before they go home — to remember for the right reasons, that is.' He gave her a tired grin.

'That sounds perfect. I can't think of a better way of putting last night firmly into the past and of enjoying our final evening together.'

'That's the idea. I hope it does the trick,' he said. He glanced up as a shower of wisteria petals, caught by a sudden light breeze, floated gracefully to the ground and rolled over and over across the paving stones until they came to rest in a heap at the foot of the table legs. The breeze died down and the terrace was still again.

He looked back at her. 'I suspect that it's going to feel very strange to you this time tomorrow with most of them on their way back to England,' he said, pushing aside the petals that had landed on the table in front of him.

'I suppose it will. But it will to you, too, after all, you've joined in all week.' She hesitated a moment. 'Has the Anderson thing made you want to return to England now?'

'Not at all. What happened with them happened, but it's no more than a blip during what's going to be a lovely summer. It's a blip that's taught me a valuable lesson about security, though, and about what's sensible and what isn't. We'll have internet access in this house next year, and there'll be no need for anyone to come across to my home.'

He picked up the teaspoon next to him and immediately put it down again. 'I think I ought to ask you the question you asked me, it's only fair. Would you prefer to go home now? If you would, you've only got to say. I'd understand. It's been traumatic for you, too. Whatever you choose to do I'll obviously pay you for the whole summer.'

His eyes were on the table as he ran his finger round the rim of the teaspoon.

She stared at his bent head. If she went back to England that weekend she might never see him again, never again feel the warmth of his gaze upon her face, the thrill of his arms around her. A lump came to her throat.

'I'm staying put,' she said, swallowing hard. 'I don't want to leave.'

His shoulders relaxed. He looked up and met her eyes across the table. 'You don't know how pleased I am to hear that,' he said quietly. 'I don't want you to leave, either. Not at all.'

Her heart stood still.

She tore her eyes away. 'So that's agreed,' she said with a half-laugh. 'We're both staying. And now I must go. I've got things to do.'

She went to stand up but he put his hand on hers to stop her, and she sat down again, her stomach jumping nervously.

'I was wondering if you'd say anything about last night — not about the theft, but about afterwards, on the drive. Despite everything that's been going on, it's been on my mind all day.'

She pulled her hand away and jumped up. 'There's nothing to say,' she said breathlessly. 'Not now, not ever. I'm sorry, I've got to go.'

He stared up at her, his face puzzled.

'I must pick out the best of the week's paintings for this evening's display,' she added.

He gestured helplessly with his hands, his palms upturned. 'You don't have to. You could follow George's example and have a rest. You can't have got much sleep last night. We don't need a display tonight, everyone would understand.'

'I want to do it. It'll help us get back to normal if we start the evening like we always do. It won't be a huge display. I'm only going to show the best of the week's work, and we haven't got the paintings done by two of our number — but I think it'll be enjoyable looking at the progress everyone's made in a week.'

'More enjoyable in some cases than others, I suspect,' he said, wryly.

'You're going to be pleasantly surprised at how you and Stephen have improved. You were sceptical at first about being able to be taught, but when you look back at your week's work, you'll see the progress you've made.'

'We shall see.'

'And when we've looked at the paintings, we can have our final *bellini* together, and then go out.'

'Fair enough, you've won me round.'

He got up. 'I'll leave you to it, then, and get back to the house. Much as I hate the thought of the bare walls and sense of violation, there are things I could be doing. With luck, the police will have gone by now and I'll be able to get on without interruption. I'll see you this evening at about seven-thirty.'

'Thank you. I'll tell the others when I next see them.'

He took a few steps, and stopped. 'I *will* have that conversation with you, Jennifer,' he said quietly, 'but at another time. We have the rest of the summer to ourselves, after all.' Then he turned, walked across the terrace and disappeared round the corner of the house.

Her stomach somersaulted. She didn't want that conversation, couldn't have it. The conversation she wanted was the one about Max and her father, not the one about Max and her. Not that there *was* a Max and her. There wasn't.

Taking a deep breath, she went resolutely into the house and over to the cupboard where she kept the work.

Kneeling down she pulled the doors open and took out the paintings and sketches that the class had done. Then she pushed the doors shut, sat down on the floor next to the pictures and started sorting them into piles.

A sudden thought hit her hard, and she drew her breath in sharply. The painting she'd been holding slipped through her fingers to the floor, unnoticed.

Her hands flew to her mouth in growing horror.

She'd turned down the chance to return to England without a second's deliberation. Not for one minute had she reasoned that she must stay close to Max in order to discover the truth about his behaviour towards her father. Not for one single second had she cast her mind back to what had happened all those years ago.

All she'd been able to think about was Max, and that she might never see him again. And that thought had torn her apart.

She felt the blood drain from her face. Oh, no, she breathed inwardly. Oh, no. How could she have done such a terrible thing? How could she have let herself fall in love with the man whose actions may have brought about the death of her father?

Because that's what she'd done — she'd fallen in love with Max.

Her vision blurring, she gazed wildly around the room. Then she covered her face with her hands and gave way to her grief.

# The Time For Truth

Standing beneath a night sky studded with glittering stars, they waved goodbye to Carlo as he drove off to his home, and then they made their way down the drive to their house. Behind them, they could hear the sound of the minibus engine gradually fading into the distance, until it was swallowed up by the still of the night.

Jennifer was the first to reach the terrace.

She'd gone through the day in a daze from the moment that she'd faced the fact that she'd fallen deeply in love with Max, and she couldn't wait for the evening to end. She needed time by herself if she was going to get on top of the feelings she shouldn't have, and bring her focus back to the reason she came to Italy.

Nick was seconds behind her. 'Come

on, you slowcoaches!' he called back up the path as he rounded the corner and on to the terrace.

'We're going slowly for a reason,' Clare said, trailing behind him, Stephen at her side. She squeezed Stephen's hand. 'We want to make the most of our last evening in Italy together, don't we, Stephen? When the evening ends, it means that the holiday's ended. We want to delay that moment for as long as possible.'

'For one ghastly minute, I thought you were going to say, 'Don't we, Stevie darling?''

Stephen glared at him, and opened his mouth to speak.

'I thought we'd banned all references, either direct or indirect, to a certain two people,' Jennifer cut in quickly.

She shook herself. She'd almost missed seeing that Nick was intent on goading Stephen, and that shouldn't have happened. She was in danger of allowing her inner anguish to over-whelm her and she mustn't do that.

The evening wouldn't go on for much longer, and when it was over, she'd have all the solitude she craved. Until then, she must keep her mind solely on the wellbeing of the group.

'*Mea culpa*, and all that,' Nick said, and he hung his head in mock shame.

She forced a bright smile to her face, and turned to Stephen and Clare. 'Anyway, it's not really goodbye for you two, is it? Your uncle tells me that you've been overcome by sudden academic fervour, Stephen, and have decided to abandon your holiday and return to England to focus on your university work. By a happy coincidence that means you'll be able to meet Clare in London at the end of next week. That's right, isn't it?'

Stephen grinned at her.

Clare smiled happily at Stephen. 'We've been working out all the details.'

'It'll be strange meeting Clare in England for the first time,' Stephen said, putting his arm around her. 'It's going to make everything much more real. What's it they say, Clare's not just for Italy, she's for ever?'

Giggling, Clare hugged him.

'Where's George?' Jennifer suddenly exclaimed. She glanced anxiously towards the path. 'I'd better go and check on him. It should have occurred to me earlier that he might need some help. He looked very tired this evening. I don't know what I was thinking of.'

She hurried back across the terrace. As she reached the foot of the path, George came into sight, leaning on Max's arm.

'Here I am, Jennifer, as you see. I fear that it's taken me a little longer than sometimes, but I'm here now. Max was good enough to aid me. I am most grateful to you, Max.'

'It was my pleasure. Come on, let's get you to a seat.'

Jennifer took George's other arm and they helped him into a chair.

'Thank you, thank you, my friends,' he said, wiping his forehead. He glanced up at Max. 'Yet another reason to be grateful to you, Max. The rest of you may not know . . . ' Max gestured that he should stop, but George held up his hand. 'No, dear boy, let me speak.' He turned to the others. 'When the waiter brought us that wonderful wine this evening, it reminded me that I'd completely forgotten the Sagrantino that our friend in Montefalco was going to bring in for me to taste today. As you can imagine, I was beside myself with annoyance that it had slipped my mind.'

'We can, indeed, imagine your consternation,' Nick murmured. Jennifer sent him a reproving glance, and he winked at her. She turned back to George.

'Don't worry, George. He'll know what's been going on,' she said. 'I'm sure that the whole of Montefalco will have known about the attempted theft before the end of the morning. You can go for your tasting session before you leave for the airport. You'll easily have enough time, your flight isn't till the afternoon.'

'There's no need, Jennifer. Max saw my concern and told me that he'd collected the wine this afternoon and that Carlo had put it in my room while we were looking at this evening's display.'

'Oh, how thoughtful of you, Max!' Jennifer exclaimed.

George nodded in agreement. 'Indeed it was. Not just a taste, but a whole bottle of a truly outstanding wine.' He looked up at Max. 'I really am most grateful. Such generosity is overwhelming.' He took a handkerchief from his pocket and wiped first one eye and then the other. 'Quite overwhelming,' he repeated, and he blew his nose.

'Stephen and I saw you in Montefalco, Max,' Clare said. 'We were looking for some things to take home, but you were walking too quickly for us to catch you up.'

'I must have been coming back from getting the wine. Did you find what you wanted?'

'Not really. I bought a few small things but nothing much was open, so I left the rest for the airport. They're bound to have some regional biscuits or something like that in the airport shop. We ended up just wandering around, and had another ice-cream from the same place as before — Stephen forgot the word for strawberry, but I remembered it.'

Jennifer glanced around the group. 'Talking of food and drink, would anyone like a tea or coffee now, or some wine? Or are you all ready to turn in? It's been a long day.'

'I don't know about the others,' Max said, 'but I think I'll go back now and have a relatively early night.'

'You showing signs of tiredness? You must be ill, Uncle!' Stephen started to laugh, then he suddenly stopped, his expression changing to one of concern. 'Come to think of it, you've been really quiet all evening, and that's not like you at all. *Are* you ill?'

'I'm fine, thanks, Stephen. I think everything's rather caught up with me at last.'

'I, too, noticed that you've not been your normal self this evening, my friend,' George remarked. 'But that is entirely to be expected. These last few days must have been a serious strain for you. It takes time to recover from such a shock, even for the strongest amongst us.'

'Just so, George,' Max said. 'Right then, Stephen. Time to go, I think. I suggest you say goodnight to Clare. She's got an early start tomorrow, and I'm sure you'll want to be up in time to see her before she goes.'

Stephen smiled down at Clare. 'I'm going to do better than that. I'm going to wave her off at the airport.'

It was impossible to tell which of them was gazing at the other more adoringly, Jennifer thought as she watched them walk along the spotlit path in the direction of the pool, their arms around each other.

George stirred in his chair, put a hand on each of its arms and made as if to rise.

At exactly the same moment, Jennifer and Max moved forward to help him.

'I, too, am going to bid you goodnight,' he said when he was on his feet. 'It's been a wonderful evening, an evening to remember, but I feel more than ready to sleep now.' He nodded briefly to Nick, gave a slight bow to Jennifer and Max, and then turned and made his way into the house.

Max went over to the edge of the terrace. 'Stephen!' he called. 'It's time we were off.'

'I suppose I ought to go, too,' Nick said.

'Ah, there you are,' Max said as Stephen and Clare came hurrying towards him. Jennifer saw that Clare's eyes were red, and she threw her a sympathetic glance.

Max turned to Clare. 'I probably won't see you tomorrow, but I expect I'll see you again in the future so there's no need for us to say goodbye.' He gave her a warm smile, put his arm around Stephen's shoulders, and the two men started walking towards the cypress trees.

Framed by the row of slender black columns that reached up to the sky, their needle tips silver in the light of the moon, Stephen kept on glancing back at Clare, who stared after them until they were lost from sight. Her eyes again filled with tears.

'Are you all right?' Jennifer asked gently.

Clare nodded. 'I'm fine, thanks. Really, I am. It's just that it's been such a wonderful week that I don't want it to end. I've loved everything about it — except for the Anderson thing, of course. But not even that could ruin it for me. I've really enjoyed the painting we've done and I've learnt masses, and I've met Stephen. I can't believe how lucky I am.'

'He obviously feels the same way. At least, about *you*, he does. I don't know about the painting,' she added with a smile.

'He says that he feels the same about me as I feel about him. But maybe he'll feel differently in England. The magic might have gone for him. That's what I'm scared about.'

'The best thing for you to do is relax and see what happens. If it's meant to be, it will be.'

'That's good advice, and I'll take it.' Clare wiped her eyes with the back of her hand. 'And what about you, Jennifer? Are you going to take your own advice?'

Jennifer looked at her questioningly. 'What do you mean?'

'We've all seen the way Max looks at you, and we've seen the way you look at him. But then you go all closed up. I don't know if you know that you're doing it, but you are. Like you said to me, shouldn't you relax and see what happens, so if it's meant to be, it can be?'

'How did an old head get on to such young shoulders?'

'Being a nurse, you hear all sorts of things. I've heard so many people say that they regret not doing things years before that they'd really wanted to do. By the time that they finally decide to do them it's nearly always too late for one reason or another. I don't want to be someone who one day, years from now, says if only. And I don't think you do, either. Or do you?'

'No, you're right, I don't,' she said slowly.

'So go for it. What have you got to lose? Anyway, I've probably said enough, if not too much, so I'll say goodnight now. I'll see you tomorrow.'

With a little wave of farewell, Clare went into the house.

Standing motionless in the middle of the empty terrace, Jennifer stared after her.

'No, I don't,' she repeated to herself, and she picked up her bag and made her way slowly back to her room.

* * *

Early the following morning she said goodbye to Clare and Nick, and a temporary goodbye to Stephen. She waved to them until the minibus was out of sight, then strolled back down the drive.

So only George was left, she thought, and not for that much longer. Max was right — it was going to feel very strange when they'd all gone. It'd be just her and Max. And Max had things he intended to say, things she didn't want to hear. A wave of ice-cold panic shot through her.

Reaching the terrace, she looked around for George. He was nowhere to be seen. She bit her lip anxiously. She'd have to find something else to do that would take her mind off her fear that Max might materialise at any moment and insist upon the conversation she was dreading.

The class's work — that would do it! She'd start sorting out the things they'd left behind. They'd taken their best pictures, carefully packaged so as not to ruin them on the journey, but not all of their earlier sketches and preliminary designs, and it had occurred to her that she might be able to make them into a collage that could be used as background to the promotional material she was going to produce. If anything could divert her thoughts, that would be it.

She went quickly to the cupboard, emptied it and spread the work out at the side of the room, as close to the patio doors as she could in order to take advantage of the best possible light. Then she knelt on the floor, her back to the glass windows, and started to put the work into piles.

A shadow passed across the room. It stopped in the path of the sun. The stream of light was cut into two.

She spun round.

Max was standing between the open patio doors, a tall dark silhouette framed by the bright sun. He stepped into the room and stared down at her, unsmiling.

Her heart in her mouth, she scrambled to her feet, brushed the dust from her jeans, and faced him.

# 'I Came Here Hating You'

He hesitated a moment, then came further into the room. 'I hope I didn't frighten you,' he said, 'turning up like this. You've gone very pale.'

'You did a bit, to be honest. Apart from George, I thought I was alone.'

'Well, you're not alone any longer. I thought I'd come across and see you.'

Her insides turned upside-down. 'I'm not sure where George is at the moment, but he'll be somewhere in the house. I'll pop along and find him if you want to hang on here.'

'I came to see *you*.' He took another step forward, then stopped, merely inches from her. Their eyes met, and locked. The air hung heavy between them.

She shivered and took a few steps back. 'Why?'

He didn't move. 'Not now, you said.

Not ever. Why, not ever?'

Her brow wrinkled. 'What do you mean?'

'I can accept the not now. We were both tired at the time. But not the not ever? Why don't you ever want to talk about what passed between us two nights ago? Something did. I felt it, and you felt it, too. I know you did.'

'I don't know what you mean.' Her voice shook.

'Yes, you do. It was there, and it was there even before that. I keep thinking back to what I saw in your eyes when we were in the minibus, waiting for the police to arrive.'

'You're mistaken. I . . . '

'I don't think I am — at least, I hope I'm not. You were genuinely afraid for me. No-one would be that afraid for someone if they didn't have strong feelings for them. They couldn't be.'

Unable to bear the sight of the hope that burned in his eyes, she looked down at the floor. 'I'd have had the same expression if a litter of puppies had been under threat,' she said weakly.

He gave her a half smile. 'And that would have been a sorry situation, too. But I rather think that this was something else. Apart from the fear for me that I saw in your eyes, I also saw a reflection of what I feel about you.'

Her eyes still rigidly fixed on the patch of floor in front of her, she shrugged her shoulders. 'I don't know what you're talking about.'

'Don't you?' he said quietly. 'Well, let me show you then.' He moved forward, put a finger lightly under her chin and raised her face to look into his. As she gazed into the fathomless depths of his darkening eyes, her knees felt weak. She let out a long low sigh and her lips parted.

'I saw this, Jennifer,' he said softly. He ran his thumb slowly along her lower lip, bent his head, and lightly brushed his lips across hers.

A wave of intense longing ran through her.

She reached out to him, and he put

his arms around her and pulled her close to him. His strength enveloped her, and her body trembled, her every nerve alive and tingling, crying out to her that she loved him, truly loved him. 'Oh, Max,' she breathed.

Oh, if only it weren't for the memory of her father, she cried inwardly, she'd want more, so very much more.

Her father!

In a panic, she pulled back from him. Her hands flew to her face. What was she thinking of, kissing the man who'd brought such misery to her family?

'Oh, no, I shouldn't have done that,' she gasped, and she stepped further back. 'I shouldn't have done that.'

'Yes, you should,' he said, his voice husky, caressing. He moved closer to her, his face full of love. Gently he pushed her hands aside and trailed his fingers down her flushed cheeks. 'It's what we both feel, what we both want.'

'It's not what *I* want,' she cried, sweeping his hands away. 'At least, I *do* want it — but I mustn't.'

His arms fell to his side. He took a step back from her, and stared at her, bewildered. 'I don't understand. What do you mean, you mustn't want it? You're not married or engaged. Nor am I. So why not?'

Tears began to roll down her cheeks.

'What is it, Jennifer? You're frightening me.'

Choking on her tears, she couldn't speak.

'I'm trying to tell you that I love you, darling Jennifer. Am I mistaken in thinking that you love me as much as I love you?'

'No. At least, I don't know.' She sobbed. 'I'm completely confused. I'm so drawn to you, you know I am. I can't stop thinking about you. Every minute of every day since I met you, you've been in my mind, and you shouldn't be. I came here hating you, and now I find myself loving you. I can't bear it, but I do. I love you so much, and I mustn't — I can't. I must leave tomorrow, or even today.'

His face went ashen. 'I don't understand what you're saying. What do you mean, you came here hating me? The first time we met was at your interview in London, so how could you hate me? If we'd met before that I know I'd remember.'

She wiped her face with the back of her hands. 'We haven't met before, not as such. But you've met my father. Maybe not you — I don't know if it was you and Peter, or just Peter.'

He frowned, and moved imperceptibly back from her. 'What's Peter got to do with any of this? He died years ago. And what do you mean, one of us met your father? You live miles away from me. I don't remember ever meeting an O'Connor before I met you.'

'O'Connor's my mother's maiden name. We started using it when we moved to Cornwall after my father died. His name was Francis Egan.'

'Francis Egan?' he said slowly. 'Yes, I remember him well. He died in somewhat tragic circumstances.' He stared hard at Jennifer. 'And you're his daughter?'

She nodded. 'Thanks to your family, he was so stressed that he had a heart attack as he was driving away from a meeting with you all. He crashed the car and was killed outright. I was only six at the time.'

'I knew he'd died in an accident, which was a terrible thing to happen, but I don't know what you mean by saying that it was thanks to my family. We did all that we could to help him. No-one could have done any more.'

'You helped him, did you?' Her voice rose. 'Like always being so late in paying for what you bought from him that he had a serious cash flow problem every month? Because of you and other companies like yours — but mainly your company as you bought so much from him — the bank finally gave up on him and called in his loan. Is that really what you call helping him?'

'You've got it wrong. That's not what happened at all.'

'Yes, it is. My mother told me. If you'd paid him when you should have done he'd never have got into such a mess, and he wouldn't have been so seriously stressed. I think that justifies my 'thanks to your family', don't you? So, you see, I won't let myself love you. I can't.'

A loud sob escaped, and she turned to walk away.

He caught her by the arm. 'But you do love me. I know that, and so do you,' he said bluntly. 'I'm sorry about your father,' he added, his voice softening, 'but you're wrong about the way we behaved towards him.'

She thrust her chin out defiantly. 'If my mother said that that's what happened, then that's what happened. Now, perhaps you'd kindly let go of me.'

He released his grip on her arm, stared at her for a moment then turned and went towards the patio doors. He reached the doors, paused, and then turned back to face her.

'No, I'm not giving up on you that easily,' he said, coming back to her. 'I'd never forgive myself if I did. I'm going to clear this up. I have to.'

'Then tell me, why did you and Peter let my father down like that? He looked on you as friends. My mother and I need to know that in order to get closure. That's why I came to Italy. Everything else that's happened just makes it all much more confusing.'

'You're confused because you love me, and you think you should hate me. Well, I'm confused, too, Jennifer.' She looked up at him, questioningly. 'I'm confused because I'm in a difficult position. I've no choice but to defend my family if I'm going to have a chance with you. But to do that, I'd have to say something hurtful about your family, and I don't want to do that. I love you and I don't want to cause you pain.'

'There's nothing you can say against them. They've not done anything wrong.'

'You're right,' he said, his voice

gentle. 'They haven't. Your mother told you something that wasn't true, but she acted out of kindness, and it's not wrong to act out of kindness. She wanted to protect someone she loved — that someone was you.'

A chill ran through her. 'What do you mean?'

'First of all, even if we and every other company had paid on time, your father would still have had a cash flow problem. It was caused by him having to pay for the goods he bought within four weeks, but everyone who bought from him had six weeks in which to pay him. It left a gap of two weeks between him paying out money and getting the money back in. That's how a lot of businesses work.'

'I know that.'

'Your father just didn't have sufficient capital behind him to cover the two weeks' gap.'

'But you made it worse, you could have . . .'

'No, Jennifer. We didn't make your

father's money troubles worse — on the contrary, Peter did everything he could to help him. Francis was a good man, and we could see that he was in trouble, so unlike most of the companies he dealt with, we didn't wait for the contractual payment date. We paid ahead of time every month.'

'You paid early?' She shook her head from side to side, disbelief in her eyes. 'I don't believe it.'

'We always did. It's something you can easily check up on if you want. It'll be in his ledgers.'

'But why did it all go wrong then? I don't understand.'

'Your father had too little capital to have set up a business on his own, especially a business of that nature. He'd have been wiser to have stayed a sales rep, which is how we first met him. However, he was desperate to have his own company, and against all advice, he went ahead, confident that it would somehow work out. And it did for a bit. The local bank manager was a friend of his and he was sympathetic to your father's problem and turned a blind eye to the two weeks' gap.'

'So what happened that made his business fail?'

'The manager was eventually moved to a different branch, as bank managers often are, and the new man was a different kettle of fish. He soon got fed up with your father's cash flow problem, wouldn't help him through it and finally called in the loan. That's what put your father on the road to bankruptcy.'

'But why did my mother say it was *your* fault?'

He hesitated, then took a deep breath. 'I don't think the collapse of his company was the only strain your father was under. There was something else, too. Please don't hate me for telling you this, but your mother had become infatuated with Peter.'

'Never,' she whispered, her face white.

'I'm sorry, but it's true. Don't blame

her too much. She was extremely young when you were born and they had very little money. It may have been that she felt trapped by everything, I don't know. But whatever it was, she made a pass at Peter.'

'She wouldn't have done.'

'I'm afraid she did. But Peter adored his wife and little boy — that was Stephen — and he made it clear that he wasn't interested in her. I think she took it quite badly. Somehow or other your father found out that your mother was keen on Peter, and he was devastated. I suspect that the stress and fear of losing not only his business, but also the wife and child he loved, was what brought about his heart attack.'

She vigorously shook her head. 'I don't believe you. Mum wouldn't lie to me.'

'What I've told you is the truth. Your mother's grief over your father's death was probably mixed up with a feeling of guilt, and perhaps also with anger at Peter's rejection. Blaming my family probably came from a combination of things.'

'I don't believe that of my mother,' she said stiffly. 'I don't believe that she'd look at someone other than my father. She loved him so much that she still hasn't got over his death. And I don't think she'd lie to me and keep on lying to me. I want you to go now, please.'

Max hesitated, then put his hand in his pocket, took out his mobile phone and set it down on the table next to the wall.

'It's up to you what you do now, Jennifer. I can understand you wanting to believe your mother, and it's only right that you should feel that way. But if, when you've had time to mull things over, you feel that you'd like to ask her to explain more fully what happened, now that you're old enough to be able to put everything into perspective, then you can use my phone. I'll leave you now, though, since that is what you clearly want.'

He went through the patio doors and across the terrace. Not once did he look back.

She stared at the place where he'd stood. 'Mum wouldn't have lied to me, she wouldn't. I just don't believe it,' she said defiantly.

Her words reverberated in the emptiness around her.

# 'Find Out What Happened'

There was a light tap and the door opened slightly. Jennifer glanced up from her seat on the floor, her face pale and tear-streaked. George's head appeared through the gap, and her heart sank.

He cleared his throat. 'Excuse me, Jennifer. I won't be in your way, will I, if I join you for a few moments? If it's not convenient, however . . . '

'Of course, you won't be in the way,' she said flatly. 'Come in.'

As he came into the room, she saw that he looked very tired, and she felt a stab of guilt at how unwelcoming she must have sounded. 'No, do come in, George. I'd be glad of the company,' she added, making a great effort to sound as if she meant it.

'Thank you, dear lady.' He closed the door behind him, went over to one of the armchairs and sat down. 'Please, don't let me interrupt you. I can see that you're busy.' He glanced down at the floor. 'It's hard to believe that we produced so much work in so little time,' he added, indicating the pictures.

'I know what you mean. It's quite impressive.' She sat back on her heels. 'To be honest, you're not really interrupting anything. I can't seem to get into the mood today. It must be the Howard and Paula factor. I still can't stop thinking about they did, or rather what they tried to do. And all the things they said to deceive us — who would have believed it of them?'

'Who indeed? Nevertheless, in the end you were cleverer than they were. It's down to you that they were caught.'

'Down to me?'

'It was you, was it not, who noticed the suitcase discrepancy? You deserve a pat on the back — you proved to be quite the detective.'

She shook her head. 'I'm not sure about that. My record for detection isn't so hot in other areas. What kind of detective accepts what they're told without question, just because it comes from their mother? Maybe when they're little, but not year after year.'

'You are being too hard on yourself, Jennifer. It's an understandable thing to do.'

'Well then, what kind of detective doesn't recognise that they're starting to feel too much for someone they shouldn't?' She shook her head and tried to laugh. 'Ignore me, George. I'm just feeling sorry for myself. How are you? Did you get all of your packing done or would you like some help?'

'Everything is done, thank you, apart from the last few things, which I shall put into my case just before I leave.' He gave a little cough and shifted his position in the chair. 'I'm afraid that I couldn't help overhearing snippets of the conversation between you and Max,' he said awkwardly. 'I do apologise, dear lady. I didn't want to hear, but I was sitting on the patio in front of my bedroom enjoying the view and the windows here were wide open.'

She stared at him in consternation. 'Oh, my goodness, I'm so sorry, George! What must you think of us — of me particularly. How very embarrassing.'

'What I think is completely unimportant, Jennifer. It's what you and Max think that matters. More than that, it's what you both feel.'

'If you heard what we said to each other, then you'll know that I've hated him all of my life, or for as long as I can remember. How could I ever love someone who might be responsible for my father's death, even if only indirectly? The answer is, I couldn't.'

'To be precise, you didn't actually hate Max — you hated what you thought he'd done. There's a great difference, if I may venture to say so. You didn't know Max other than through your mother's words. When you met the man himself and got to know him, you fell in love with the man you found him to be. Now that you know he's innocent of any wrongdoing — and I think you do know that in your heart, do you not — you are free to love him. Is that not so?'

'It isn't as simple as that. Part of me desperately wants to believe him, and part of me doesn't. If Max is telling the truth, then my mother isn't. Even if I could accept that she lied at the time of my father's death, I could never think it acceptable that she carried on lying for so many years.'

'Would it not be an idea to call your mother and talk to her?' he suggested gently. 'It seems unlikely that you will be able to leave matters as they are now, not if you want any peace of mind. Max has left you his telephone expressly for that purpose.'

She glanced towards the mobile phone. 'I suppose I could, couldn't I?' Then she looked back at George. 'But again, it's not that straightforward, is it? If Mum *has* lied to me and I force her to confess, I'll humiliate her, and I wouldn't want to do that. She is my mother, after all, and she's always been a wonderful mother.'

'It is possible, my dear girl, that your mother has been unhappy for years about the lie she'd felt obliged to tell and to keep on telling. She may welcome a momentary humiliation if it means putting an end to the deception.'

'But no-one *made* her do anything. She could have told me the truth from the very start.'

He raised his eyebrows. 'Indeed? I am trying to imagine how a young mother would tell her six-year-old daughter, who had just lost her father, that the advances she'd made to another man had added to the father's stress to such an extent that he'd suffered a heart attack. It's hard to see how such a revelation could help the daughter in her time of grief, and at a time when all she had left was her mother. No, far better to blame it on someone else, I would have thought.'

She stared at him. 'When you put it

like that, I suppose I can see that it would be difficult. But surely she could have told me the truth when I got older — if what Max has said *is* the truth.'

'I suspect that the longer you live with a lie, the harder it is to rectify it. There may never have seemed a right time to come clean, as they say. Nor any reason for her to do so. And your mother may even have come to believe that what she told you was the truth.'

'I suppose that's possible.'

'As Max said, her first thought will have been for you, Jennifer. Don't be too hard on her — she will have had your welfare at heart when she decided to say what she did.'

'What you say does make sense. I can see that,' she said slowly.

'Be that as it may, I am sure that neither what I say, nor what Max has said, will be sufficient to undo a belief that you have held for many years. If you are to rid yourself of what I suspect has now become an unwelcome burden, my dear, you will have to speak to the one person who knows better than anyone else what really took place.' He gestured towards the table. 'The means to do so is there. And as it so happens,' he said, rising awkwardly to his feet, 'I need to check again that I haven't left anything in the wardrobe. So if you will excuse me, Jennifer, I'll leave you now.'

She jumped up, went quickly to the door and held it open for George. As he started to walk past her, she leaned across and kissed him lightly on the cheek. 'Thank you, George. I'm so glad that you were sitting where you were and overheard what we said.'

He paused. 'Dear lady,' he said, gently. 'Find out what happened. When you know this, you'll be free to go and love your man, and if you have a fraction of the happiness with Max that I had with my Agnes, you're going to be a very happy lady indeed.' He inclined his head towards her and went through the doorway into the hall.

She closed the door behind him,

leaned back against it for a moment, then walked over to the table and picked up Max's phone. Her fingers hovered briefly above the keys, and then she started to tap out a number she knew by heart.

# The Painful Truth

The late morning sun was beating down on the garden as Jennifer pushed the patio doors wide open and went out on to the terrace. Still clutching the mobile phone in her hand, she stood in the shade beneath the awning and stared around her.

Beneath the deep blue sky, the glossy green and purple sheen of the garden was broken only by the vibrant hues of the plants nestling amid the verdant foliage and by the brightly coloured flowers that overflowed the large terracotta tubs placed around the edge of the terrace.

A light breeze swept across the garden, ruffling the ferns and the bushes. Through the gently swaying fronds, the pool could be glimpsed, its clear blue water sparkling in the light of the sun.

She breathed in deeply and inhaled the scent of lavender and rosemary.

What a morning it had been.

It had been achingly difficult to bring up a subject so sensitive with her mother — the person who'd loved and cared for her all of her life, and who'd done all that she could to help her fulfil her every dream. At first, her questions had been hesitant and embarrassed, but gradually they'd gathered speed until they were pouring out of her, tumbling one after the other, demanding to be answered.

Her mother's initial reaction had been one of shocked surprise and she'd rushed to deny everything that Max had claimed, insisting that her original account had been the right one.

She'd wanted to stop there, to accept without further question her mother's words, but she couldn't. Her every instinct told her that only by probing more deeply, hateful though it was to do so, would she find out the part that Max had played in their misery. If he had played any part in it at all. She had to know this.

She'd challenged her mother again. Once more her mother had vigorously begun to deny everything, but all of a sudden, she'd stopped mid-sentence. There'd been a moment's silence, and then she'd started to speak again, her voice somehow different this time, and Jennifer had heard from her mother the account that she'd first heard from Max.

From then on, her mother had seemed unable to stop talking, and she'd poured out the whole story amid profuse apologies and tears of regret mingled with relief. It was as if Jennifer had unlocked the door to something that had been desperate to escape for a very long time.

Her mother hadn't attempted to defend herself — quite the opposite, in fact. She'd told Jennifer that there was nothing she could say that could justify blaming a family who had done all that they could to help her father. Eaten up by guilt at the time of his death, the idea of putting all the blame on the Castaniens had come to her in a flash. She'd thought it wouldn't matter what she said as she and Jennifer were moving away and they were unlikely ever to meet the family again.

Once she'd started accusing them, she hadn't seen a way of stopping. Jennifer had loved her father deeply and had wanted to keep his memory alive, and she had wanted this, too, so they'd talked frequently over the years about what had happened, always using the original version of the events. It had never occurred to her that Jennifer might one day seek out the Castaniens to discover why they'd acted in the way she'd been told that they had.

She could now see how wrong she'd been, and that she should have told her the truth years before, and she'd finished up by begging Jennifer to forgive her and not to let their relationship be damaged by the revelations. Then she'd fallen silent, waiting.

'I can understand why you did it,' Jennifer had told her. 'And there's nothing to forgive. In your place I probably would have done the same. You acted as you did out of love.' And they had both broken down.

'I've been hating myself for lying to you for so long now,' her mother had told her through her tears. 'You don't know how pleased I am that everything's out in the open at last. I feel I can now move on.'

'We both can.'

'I never thought I'd hear myself saying this, but I'm glad you went to work for Max Castanien, Jenny. I only saw him once. He was very young then, of course, but he seemed a nice lad. What's he like now?'

Jennifer's heart had given a sudden lurch, and she'd bit her lip. If her relationship with Max survived their exchange of words that morning, and if it developed in the future — a huge if, but she desperately hoped that it would — she couldn't just spring it upon her mother without having given her at least some indication of how she felt about him.

'Actually, Mum,' she'd begun nervously. 'I ought to . . .'

But her mother had spoken across her. 'It's all right, Jennifer,' she'd said. 'I know you so well that I'm picking up on what you're trying to tell me. I'm not saying that it would ever be easy to meet a Castanien again, of course it wouldn't. So many memories are attached to that family, but if he's the right man for you, then you'll have my blessing. It's the very least you deserve.'

'Oh, Mum,' Jennifer breathed, and a weight lifted from her shoulders. A lump came to her throat. 'Thank you.'

Soon after that, they'd said goodbye, having promised to speak again in a day or two, and she'd wandered out on to the terrace in a daze.

She stepped out from under the awning, put her face up to the sun and let its warmth flow through her. Something tickled her toes and she glanced down. A breeze had blown a smattering of white rose petals across her toes. Her eyes followed the petals as they lightly skimmed the surface of the patio and drifted over the grass to the cypress trees.

She turned to face the trees and to face the house where Max would be, and she knew that she absolutely had to see him. She had to see him that instant. Not the following day, not later that day, but just as soon as she possibly could. She found herself taking a step forward, and another, and another.

By the time that she reached the trees, she was running.

Not wanting to waste a precious moment by going up the slope to the linking path, she sped through the nearest gap in the line of trees and ran straight across the grass to the *loggia*.

One thought filled her mind, and that thought was Max.

No matter what he felt about her now that he knew why she'd come there, she had to tell him that she was desperately sorry for what she'd said, for what she'd done, and that she loved him with all her heart. Even if she was too late and her feelings were thrown back in her face, she still had to tell him.

By the time she was close to the house she was panting heavily, and she slowed down to a walk as she stepped on to the *loggia*. The French windows suddenly opened and Max came out.

She stopped sharply, and involuntarily stepped back.

Standing motionless in the shadow thrown by the pillar, her eyes followed him as he walked to the edge of the *loggia*, his hands in his pockets, leaned against the pillar nearest to him and gazed at the view in front of him.

He had never looked more handsome, she thought, in his open-necked grey shirt, his sleeves rolled up to his elbows, his face and forearms lightly tanned.

And he had never looked more sad and dejected.

Squinting against the sun, he glanced up at the sky and then again stared ahead of him.

With a sigh, he straightened up, turned slightly and caught sight of her.

An expression of surprise swept across his face. He pulled his hands from his pockets and took a step towards her.

She stood staring at him, rooted to the spot, her heart racing as he walked towards her, gathering speed, his eyes asking a question.

He reached her and stopped. For a moment neither said a word.

Then she held out his mobile phone. 'I thought I ought to return your phone,' she said, breaking into the silence, her voice coming from somewhere far away.

His eyes on her face, he took the phone and put it in his pocket. And waited.

'I'm sorry, Max. Everything you said was true. My mother's told me about Peter and her — not that there ever was a Peter and her.' Her voice caught in her throat. 'I'm so sorry.'

'So you *did* call her. I wasn't sure if you would, and I didn't know if she'd tell you the truth if you did.'

'I knew in my heart that what you said was true, but I had to hear it from her. I don't know why I did, but I did. I'm sorry.'

His dark brown eyes gazed down at her, warm with sympathy. 'There's nothing for you to feel sorry about. You did what any loyal daughter would do.'

'I still feel as if I let you down.' She took a deep breath. He made a move as if to speak. 'No, don't say anything, Max. I must say this while I've got the courage to do so,' she added, her words falling over themselves. 'I wouldn't blame you if you hated me, but even if you do, I have to tell you that I love you. I love you so much that it hurts. I can't bear to think of life without you.'

His face broke into a broad smile, and he threw back his head. 'Yes!' he cried out to the sky, and he reached out to her and pulled her close to him. 'I could never hate you, Jennifer. I love you far too much for that.' And he buried his face in her hair.

'Despite everything?' she asked, her voice lost on the folds of his shirt.

'Definitely despite everything. This morning's been sheer hell. I thought I might have lost you for ever. I never want to feel like that again. The houses, the paintings, my company — nothing means anything if you can't share it with the person you love. And from the moment I met you, *you* have been the person I love. Without you, my life would be empty.'

She gazed up at him in naked relief. 'Oh Max, when you left, I was so unhappy. I thought that you wouldn't want me any more.'

'Not want you?' He pulled slightly back from her and gazed down into her face with a passion that took her breath away. 'I shall always want you. You say that you can't bear to think of life without me, well I know that I can't bear to think of life without you. There's only one thing for it. Will you marry me, Jennifer?'

'Oh, yes, I will!' she cried. 'I love you! Now that I can finally say it, I feel so free. And so very, very happy. I don't deserve to be this happy.'

'Yes, you do.' His lifted his hand and lightly traced the arch of her brow, the line of her nose, the fullness of her lips, the curve of her chin. Then he took her face in his hands and stared down at her, his eyes ablaze with love.

'I've many beautiful pictures at home in England,' he said, his voice full of wonder, 'and I've many beautiful pictures on the walls here, but nothing comes remotely close to how beautiful you are to me. You are a picture that I'll never tire of looking at, and I'm the luckiest person alive to be able to do so every day for the rest of my life.'

A low sigh of sheer bliss escaped her, and she raised herself on her toes, brought her lips to his and silenced him.